Eric Morales

FERNANDO A. FLORES

Valleyesque

Fernando A. Flores was born in Reynosa, Tamaulipas, Mexico, and grew up in South Texas. He is the author of the collection *Death to the Bullshit Artists of South Texas* and the novel *Tears of the Trufflepig*, which was long-listed for the Center for Fiction First Novel Prize and named a Best Book of 2019 by Tor.com. His fiction has appeared in *Ploughshares*, the *Los Angeles Review of Books Quarterly Journal, frieze, Grand Journal, Porter House Review,* and other publications. He lives in Austin, Texas.

ALSO BY FERNANDO A. FLORES

Death to the Bullshit Artists of South Texas

Tears of the Trufflepig

VALLEYESQUE

Valleyesque

STORIES

Fernando A. Flores

MCD × FSG ORIGINALS

FARRAR, STRAUS AND GIROUX   NEW YORK

MCD × FSG Originals
Farrar, Straus and Giroux
120 Broadway, New York 10271

These stories previously appeared, in slightly different form, in the following publications: Hingston & Olsen's *2019 Short Story Advent Calendar* ("The Science Fair Protest"), *Construction* ("Nocturne from a World Concave"), *New Border Voices: An Anthology* ("The 29th of April"), *Porter House Review* ("Zapata Foots the Bill"), *Ploughshares* ("Nostradamus Baby"), the *Los Angeles Review of Books Quarterly Journal* ("Possums"), *Conflict of Interest* ("Panchofire & Marina"), *frieze* ("El Ritmo de la Noche"), *Grand Journal* ("Pheasants"), and *Wander* ("The Oswald Variations").

Title-page art and hand-lettering by Na Kim.

Library of Congress Cataloging-in-Publication Data
Names: Flores, Fernando A., 1982– author.
Title: Valleyesque : stories / Fernando A. Flores.
Description: First edition. | New York : Farrar, Straus and Giroux, 2022. | "MCD × FSG Originals."
Identifiers: LCCN 2021057146 | ISBN 9780374604134 (paperback)
Subjects: LCGFT: Short stories.
Classification: LCC PS3606.L5886 V35 2022 | DDC 813/.6—dc23
LC record available at https://lccn.loc.gov/2021057146

Designed by Abby Kagan

www.fsgoriginals.com • www.fsgbooks.com
Follow us on Twitter, Facebook, and Instagram at @fsgoriginals

10 9 8 7 6 5 4 3 2 1

For the RGV exiles, and exiles living in the RGV

The Valley is a place where the new anti-life force is breaking through. Death hangs over the Valley like an invisible smog. The place exerts a curious magnetism on the moribund. The dying cell gravitates to the Valley . . . The Valley was desert, and it will be desert again.

—WILLIAM S. BURROUGHS

Shut up—get the fuck away from me!

—MARC HARDCORE

CONTENTS

VALLEYESQUE

QUESO

Watching the news on television, Marcos yelled, "That anchor's face ain't real," and hurled an empty glass. The glass bounced off the TV screen and, curiously, neither shattered. Pissed as hell, he walked to the kitchen and brushed his teeth over the sink.

It rained as he got on the bus and Marcos scanned his found student ID that let him ride for free.

At the job interview the general manager asked him to describe his talents and ambitions in the most creative, non-misogynist way, and explain why she should give him the job.

Marcos said to her, "Willie was the only other Mexican in east Kingsville, and one day he held a ripe red orange to a butcher's nose and made him describe the smell of the motherland on his fingers. The butcher was also Mexican, of no relation."

"Very good," said the general manager, marking off a box

in her notes. "Now, here at this job we are a tightly knit community. On a scale of one to ten, how would you describe your collaboration with others upon encountering a tough situation?"

"Well, first you wring the neck of the big turkey till it flops. Then you make a soup from the rest and feed it to the others, slowly watching them eat, greedily offering them more water and more bread. Wait until afterward to bring up their sisters and the war."

"Excellent, Mr. Marcos. And, using the same scale of one to ten, tell me something you think you could improve, either in your work ethic or personal integrity."

"There's nothing safer than a shark to ride. Tape notes under the table, I'll learn the ropes, the insides and outsides of this trade. Just give me the chance and I'll have a mind for the books and how to make money disappear. Piles will wheelbarrow out the back or from the bottle and you'll never even know. Then I'll bring the horses in and forget about it. Gimme the pies, give 'em."

"All right, Mr. Marcos. Looks like we got what we need. Thank you so much for the opportunity to interview you. We'll get back to you by the end of the day."

When the boss read the application he thought out loud to himself, "All I want is to have a place where anybody can just walk right in and order a bowl of melted cheese. And we'll throw in some spices for flavor. They'll be served with hardened, broken tortillas. Chips, we'll call them. And people can dip the hardened tortilla chips into this melted cheese when they're having a good time. We'll call the cheese queso. Not pronounced Mexican, but 'kay-so.' The trick, I've learned from the best, is that you gotta co-opt their culture. Hijack it, and sell them back a cheaper version. An authentic experience that's better, faster than the real thing. We'll also make our version of what they call breakfast tacos, and serve them round the clock. To save time, the tortillas will be pre-made. Possibly purchased in bulk and at a discount from a provider. The eggs, they'll have to be already cracked in a container, and poured on the grill upon getting ordered. This touch is important. It is what will let us advertise them as 'fresh.' Every taco will also come sprinkled with cheese. Unless otherwise specified, the standard is that every taco will be topped off with this cheese. American. And just shredded over, but pre-shredded, also. The American cheese will have to be pre-shredded. Yes. That goes without saying. And this young man, he's going to be the one grilling them. We'll start him on the graveyard shift and take it from there."

THE SCIENCE FAIR PROTEST

When the new gangsters got elected and took control, atoms could no longer be said to be the smallest form of matter. So anytime you sawed off a hunk of wood and chopped it to its smallest possible point, it could no longer be said that you'd made an atom out of wood, but instead, Wow, *that hunk of wood is now beyond microscopic.*

Now, I'm no science teacher, but one of my neighbors at the time was, and the second night of the Science Fair Protest he came knocking on my screen door with a case of beer from across the border, which I found odd because I'd never known him to be a drinker.

"Efe," he said, "I have to ask for a huge favor. I'm meeting someone who's bringing me a document I need. We're making a trade for this case of beer. I'm thinking it's too risky at my place. Can they come over here, you think?"

I didn't see the harm in it, but first asked what kind of document he was expecting.

"You'll see," he said.

My neighbor's name was Ram. He taught biology to eighth graders at Bexar Middle School and was around my age. I'll never get used to anybody my age being a teacher; we always seem to have a lot more growing up to do ourselves.

The clamor and hooting crackled from the streets as if from a distant forest fire—for all we knew something really *could've* caught fire. Then, as if reading my mind, Ram said, "I'm glad these protests have been for the most part peaceful."

Twenty-five minutes or so later a young man in a backward cap and baggy clothes knocked on my screen door. He was with a woman—the tallest woman I'd ever seen. Taller than me, and I'm over six feet. She was stylish and made-up like she was going clubbing, but maybe she dressed this way always, in a gray miniskirt and shiny black shoes. Under her partner's arm was a very conspicuous brown bag, and, standing below the seventy-five-watt light bulb hanging from my clicking ceiling fan, he pulled out a shrink-wrapped vinyl record. It was an original pressing of an album by seventies music sensation Xavier Felipe, known in certain circles of jukebox pop as the Mexican Neil Diamond. The record was his fourth release, titled after its hit single, "Volver a Vivir."

I pulled out all the milk crates and chairs for my guests, before dusting off the record player and fiddling with the wonky stylus. Ram started getting jumpy when I couldn't figure out how to tighten it, so he requested to give it a try.

"Your screwdriver is too big," he said. Ram was getting nervous and sweaty, as Charlie, the young man, cracked open a beer for himself and Verona, the extremely tall woman.

When Verona saw we were having a hard time, she asked what the problem was, and, using a tiny screwdriver from a wooden case in her handbag, she tightened the stylus, started up the machine, and slid the record onto it. The opening chords of the first track were a glorious moment, and Ram and I expressed our gratitude to her.

The four of us sat in my tiny living room drinking and listening to Xavier Felipe like he'd suddenly become our religion. As the beers continued popping, we kept turning over the record. Though I was the only one who really spoke Spanish, the four of us learned all the songs as we got drunker, and they gradually became very personal to us.

Ram's energy began to dim, and as we got another suitcase of beer going he was the first to get political when he said, "These new gangsters, I don't know about them, Efe. They want to change the way everyone thinks."

This is true, I remember saying to myself. It was easy for me to forget, being wrapped up in my own life, but now that the new gangsters had come into power, Ram had a lot to lose, with him being an instructor of science—biology, no less, which had recently become a very open target in the discourse with the new gangsters. I tried to think of something intelligent I could say, and like a fool asked how this would affect his curriculum.

"Get this," he said. "Instead of having regular lab hours once a week, we are going to have class outside on a field and play this game called Stick and Ball. Are you familiar? It's when you have a stick, and not really a ball, but a big rock. And with one hand you throw the rock in the air, and with the one holding the stick you try to whack it. As far as you can."

I don't know why, but hearing this, I was rather impressed that biology—a class I'd had to take at least twice in my limited academic life—was being replaced with this Stick and Ball game.

Once Ram finally got the politics talk out of his system, we all kept getting drunker while the Mexican Neil Diamond lived up to his name—that rugged voice, hinting at a working-class background; his catchy hooks and backing wall of session musicians, who probably doubled as hired killers. The four of us sang out loud, then took turns standing in the middle of the living room, each of us doing our best impression and lip-synching to Xavier Felipe.

I took advantage of the fact that we were at my place and got smashed and somewhere along the way blacked out. When I came to, everything was silent, my screen door was wide open, and on my floor were the young man and Verona dry humping and making out. I crept into my room, shut the door, and before passing out again imagined myself throwing a rock into the air, and with a stick trying to hit it.

Walking home after stocking cans overnight, I ran into a couple of youngsters by an alley, pointing, throwing rocks, and in a strange way mocking a nest of squawking grackles.

I'd been on edge during that walk because, originally, I had been hired to stock produce at the market, not cans. The feeling of touching only cold aluminum cans for hours and hours had left me uneasy. I'd told my supervisors I had this particular problem, but there was nothing they could do, because our shipments of produce had been reduced by 75 percent since the takeover by the new gangsters. Prices of everything had gone up; regularly scheduled shipments had a coin toss's chance of even arriving. Nobody was happy. The canned-goods shipments, however, were always on time, and I helped my coworkers unload and shelve them until things got closer to normal.

The rim of the sky was like wet clay slowly hardening into ceramic.

One of the youngsters was yelling at the grackles, "Avis-pas, avispas," the Spanish word for "bees." The youngster was blond, and his two friends were as brown as me. A grackle, the one that resembled a football the most, flew down, and in a flash—like it was a heist they'd rehearsed many times—the blond kid threw a rock up into the air, and, using a stick, one of the brown kids whacked it. The rock projectiled into the path of the football grackle and knocked it down.

The youngsters laughed and celebrated as they ran toward the motionless grackle on the ground. The blond kid picked it up, then all three of them went running down Reynolds Street. I quickened my pace and followed them as people walked around us and asked me questions I half heard. After a couple of blocks I thought I'd lost them, but then spotted them knocking at the door of an old blue house.

An elderly man answered the door and eyed the youngsters very suspiciously. It was obvious he didn't quite trust them. The man inspected the grackle skeptically, then out of his pocket gave each of them a rust-colored coin.

I projected my frustrations onto this man, and waited until the youngsters turned the corner and disappeared into the cityscape before I walked toward that same door and knocked three times, like the youngsters had.

The elderly man answered the door. He had a sniveling look, like he was ready to bite my neck, when I said to him, "Hey, you got these boys running grackles for you?"

"What?" he said.

"I saw what just happened here," I told him, "and I don't like the influence you're having on these youngsters."

"That's because you've never had grackle soup," he said. "See?"

He invited me inside, and I didn't see a reason to decline. In his kitchen there was a basket of plucked grackle feathers with bloody tips and a filmy smell of boiling raw meat in the air.

"I'm gonna send you home with a little container of soup. No need to bring the container back to me. Just keep the soup in your refrigerator and heat it up in a pot normally. It keeps well, so you can also freeze it and save it for another season."

Taking the plastic receptacle with grackle soup from the man, I said, "Okay."

I walked out of his house, down the streets that would take me home. I felt somewhat irresponsible for having taken soup from this complete stranger, especially one who had kids running grackles. Instead of flushing the soup down the toilet, which is what I had been prepared to do, I stored it in my empty freezer.

In a way, I concluded, these kids were more advanced than my generation had been at their age. What they'd done to get that grackle to hit the ground took some serious skills. It'd been a very coordinated and impressive operation.

Ram, who had once been just a casual, neighborly acquaintance, became something of a friend of mine. I got to know him pretty well, and, in turn, I told him a couple of things about myself I hadn't told anyone, like the fact that I was still waiting to become a naturalized citizen. Ram was one of those types who cared a lot about his career, and had a passion for wanting to teach biology to teenagers that was admirable even to me.

"I guess I take it for granted," I said to him once, "that as kids we were taught the parts of plant and animal cells, and that there is a solar system, and such."

He told me the outer space curriculum was unaffected by the learning policies the new gangsters had implemented—it was only teaching about the way life on this planet grew that had been changed.

I'd lost count of which day of the Science Fair Protest we were in, but on my walk home from work one morning the streets were packed with protesters—the sidewalks were so congested that when I got to Rodgers Street, I had to step aside and figure out a game plan for getting home.

Across the flow of people somebody was waving their arm comically in the air, and I recognized this person as Sheila, a former coworker at the market who one day had just stopped showing up for her shifts. At first I was amazed anybody would recognize me in this stream of people. Then Sheila started signaling in a way I interpreted to mean that we were to meet in the middle of the street and march along with the protesters. Mechanically, I put out my cigarette and joined her.

We didn't even say hello to each other. People had different chants I couldn't make out, while kettle drums blasted from many hollows within the crowd of protesters.

"Do you know what is going on here?" I yelled.

She shook her head and, looking right at me, yelled, "No. I stopped watching the news and keeping up a while back."

"Me as well!"

We marched along together for a bit, then got sucked through different pockets of the crowd and I never saw Sheila again.

I regretted making it a habit to have drinks with Ram and finally had to tell him the truth—my body just couldn't take a beating like the ones I gave it throughout my twenties.

He got the hint and stopped dropping by. We were still on good terms, however, and always had a short conversation when we met in the courtyard of our complex. One evening, on a walk after an encounter with Ram like this, I turned down Daffodil Avenue, where a small crowd had gathered in front of Al's Smoke Shop. They had formed a half-moon between the street and the door of the shop, and, amazed and silent, the throng looked upon two grown men in a fistfight. The men were agitated with anger and spitting insults at each other.

When it was apparent that nobody would intervene, my heart raced, and as I watched I noticed the men weren't really trying to hurt each other, or, if they were, they had never been in a fistfight in their lives. They both looked awkward and out of shape. One of them wore a T-shirt and slacks, while the other man was dressed as if he worked in a fancy office building.

As one of the spectators standing in the half-moon, I looked around to see if the cops were coming, or if anybody found this brawl as humorous as I did. When it got boring and I was thinking about leaving, I asked a woman carrying a grocery bag, who had been standing there before me, why these two were fighting.

She responded, "They disagree about the Dreyfus Affair."

The man in the T-shirt slugged the office man on his ear, and he screamed like something in there had ruptured.

"Which one do you think will win?" I asked her, and as I walked away she said, "Hard to tell at the moment."

Since I'd cut back on the drinking, walking city block after city block with no direction was how I spent most of my free time. As dusk crawled out that evening, I couldn't get this incident out of my head—I mean, I knew the new gangsters and the Science Fair Protest had stirred up many feelings in everybody, but getting into a fistfight about the Dreyfus Affair, more than a hundred years later and here, far away from France, seemed ridiculous. What came to mind for me most was the work of Marcel Proust titled À *la recherche du temps perdu*. Though I'd never read the book, I knew the Dreyfus Affair played an important peripheral role in the narrative.

I tried to recall the facts I knew about Proust, picturing him more as a mythical figure that passes in some way through people's lives than as a writer. I knew he'd written this more-than-four-thousand-page saga that takes place in only about three allotted days; that he was in love with Albertine, and also deeply tortured by her.

During this walk I began to fear something absurd. I began to fear that if, for whatever reason, I finally sat down and read Proust, this scene I'd experienced with the street fight would be a passage therein—that the reality of Proust's narrative had somehow been translated into my own, or maybe the other way around.

But who is the character of me all along? I wondered. And who is Swann here?

Back in my room, I wasn't eager to go to bed or for a new day. The market warehouse changed my work schedule and I was no longer working night shifts. My record player had broken and I'd accumulated fees at the public library, so I hadn't had new books to read in a minute.

I wasn't surprised when Ram knocked on my screen door that night, and, with a feeling of relief, I welcomed him in. When I asked him what was up, Ram said, "Look what they gave us today," and held out a regular-sized hammer.

"Who gave this to who?"

"Who do you think? The new gangsters. They sent us a box of them. Teachers are to give one hammer to every student. That's actually our new education motto: 'A hammer for every student.' They're also streamlining my science curriculum to include building projects year-round. Hear those people protesting out there? I just came over here from joining them. Wanted to hit you up about it earlier, but you seemed busy. What's up with you?"

I recounted to him my earlier incident with the street fight and what had led to my spiral of thinking about the Dreyfus Affair and Proust—whom, it turned out, Ram hadn't read either. This fact seemed to upset him. He stamped his feet and pouted, cursed this and that about the old and the new gangsters; then a vision must have struck him, because, pointing one finger at the wall for no reason, he said, "You know what must've happened? The reality Proust created in that book leaked into *your* reality. Do you see what that occurrence implies? It implies that there are similar leaks happening to other people's lives all the time. Flannery O'Connor might be leaking down on a teenage girl at the park, or Pérez Galdós is leaking into a pensioned widower's life. Daphne du Maurier, maybe, is leaking into somebody

pumping gas at a station by a motel, or that story by Haw-
thorne about people throwing the world into a big fire, so we
can cheer and heckle as it burns, is leaking into . . . I don't
know—"

"The life of a new gangster."

"One of the new gangsters, yes. The only possible answer. Do you think that once you've created a literary landscape, that landscape will be forever leaking back into the
world? Even if one has never read this author—these people
who don't read are probably the ones who suffer the most
leaks into their lives, actually. But then what does that say
about our own lives, yours and mine? Those of us that are
familiar with these authors and these works?"

Ram stood up, and this time he was pointing at something else—he was pointing at the sound we'd grown accustomed to, the sound of the Science Fair Protest making the
rounds of the town. "Whose literary reality is this," he continued, "that is leaking into our lives? The obvious answer is
Orwell's. But, no. It's gotta be a writer nobody's ever heard
of, hunkered in a cabin somewhere, or in some tenement
house. What sweet, miserable poet's story is leaking into our
reality today? If only. If only the leaks were visible. That way
we could plug them up. With cork or our dirty rags."

After this exchange, Ram went on his way and I dropped
the whole issue with Proust and the Dreyfus Affair.

The following day I awoke to a strange sensation that
something had happened. Not to me, but somewhere out in

the world. Something that would alter the landscape of our lives even more.

I refrained from reading the news, made coffee, and had the last of the bananas I'd kept frozen. A cool fall breeze came through my screen door, and from another apartment I could hear somebody playing bad pop music loudly. But I didn't mind. I was even grateful.

At the market, all of us working in the warehouse cheered when the first truck of produce in almost a month backed up against the dock. Most of the produce was in great condition, and I spent the majority of my shift stocking the store as people picked items for their rationed amounts.

On my way home I had the feeling of being a piece in a board game—the streets and avenues were all replicas of pieces in a board game as well, along with the vehicles and the pedestrians wearing their headphones, rarely making eye contact. I was looking down at the ground, imagining the rules of this game, when through my peripheral vision I saw a tall figure, wearing the unmistakable Doxie's Coffee uniform, walking toward me. I was startled when this person grabbed me by the shoulders and turned me to make direct eye contact. As other pedestrians walked around us, this person let go of my shoulders, struck a pose, and right there broke out singing a catchy verse I recognized from Xavier Felipe's hit single "Volver a Vivir," in an accent that gave away they weren't fluent in Spanish.

I clapped and said, "Oh, shit."

Even before I read her name tag, I knew this person was Verona, the tall woman I'd partied with back at my place.

We talked about how fun that night had been, then she said, "I'm on my way to work."

"Oh yeah? I just got out myself."

"You work at Sobie's Market, right? Are you guys hiring there, by any chance?"

"No," I told her, "we are not right now," even though I knew there were a few openings.

Somehow it seemed appropriate for a person like me to work at Sobie's Market, but I could see better things for Verona; having her as my coworker would feel like some kind of injustice. She noticed my grocery bag and yelled, "Is that a banana? I haven't seen any in weeks."

I gave her a couple from my bunch and we parted ways without exchanging information.

Walking down the sidewalk, I pictured her both ways I'd encountered her: in a Doxie's Coffee work uniform, and ready to party and get down, dry humping on my floor. Through no choosing of my own, I wondered what kinds of things she did day-to-day. I imagined her reading a book, or maybe writing fiction—and maybe some of it leaking here and there, into our real world.

As I turned into my neighborhood the sun looked like a bowling ball cracked in half. I listened to the streets growing louder, and asked myself how many days into the Science Fair Protest we actually were.

NOCTURNE FROM A WORLD CONCAVE

Frédéric Chopin awoke wearing his clothes and muddy shoes and feeling the cold slobber of the orange sun dripping down his face—he didn't know if it was rising or setting, and let out a gnarled walrus groan. He struggled off his cot, unsure what getting up or doing anything really meant, then remembered the money. He pulled out the wad from his trench coat: old green dollars mixed with colorful pesos. He thought to count it, but it looked like all of it. Most of it.

Like a selfish, needy friend who drops in when never wanted, the retching arrived: one, two, three dry heaves, the third one long and pronounced and painful, and for a moment Chopin thought his organs had finally hatched their escape from his slopped-up insides. He made it to the toilet and the red sprayed in chunks and pellets, most of it settling on the seat.

Chopin brushed his teeth, washed his face, combed his hair, and grabbed the yellow customs papers tacked to the wall by the door. He exited his apartment and climbed down the steep staircase, clutching the railing with his right hand.

He landed on the sidewalk off Plaza Bonifacio near the market square of Ciudad Juárez. Hunched over, Chopin was still taller than all the people moving by him—the people that moved by him every day, and that once upon a time had even greeted him. Though he felt himself a ghost now, it was when people smiled or acknowledged him that he feared they must know more than they should of his soul—or that maybe they were familiar with his music. It seemed that just a few years prior people had been different; they were more bothersome when he was trying to start his day. But now people hardly said hello or made eye contact, which to him was no problem, really.

He spotted the kids on the bright side of the street, saw them pointing in his direction and laughing, and muttered to himself, "God, these damned kids want what's left of my blood," and he accelerated his pace. The kids (there were three of them—siblings: two boys, one girl), in their off-colored clothes, ran like they were dancing through the traffic, cabs, *peseras*, and people along the border. They cornered Chopin, despite his efforts to sneak past, and started chanting, "Papá Chopin! Papá Chopin!"

The elder boy was selling bags of chicharróns and fried chips, the girl was selling Chiclets, and the younger boy was selling nothing at all but held his hand out, begging for alms.

Chopin waved one arm briskly but slowly, like he was shooing off large prehistoric insects.

"Not now, kids," Chopin growled. "Papá Chopin's gotta make rent—"

"*Papá Chopin*," the elder boy said, "*nada más lo que pueda, para mi guitarra . . . quiero tocar la guitarra como usted toca el piano. Órale, señor, porfa . . .*"

Chopin ignored the kids and hurried off. It was the only way to get rid of them, and he didn't feel bad doing so, knowing that the good he'd done for them made up for these minuscule encounters.

With his left hand he felt the rubber band around the wad of money in his coat pocket and continued a few more blocks along Plaza Bonifacio, before turning left on Calle 6 de Mayo.

Chopin asked himself what month it could be, then remembered it, along with the year, and he chuckled with his mouth closed. All at once he realized that his shoes were soaked, that it had rained the night before, and that his mother was still dead.

"Goddammit," he said, then muffled his cough with his coat sleeve.

Chopin had buried his mother the previous week, but when he thought about it, he had no idea what the term "previous week" meant. She was dead, though. Spared living past the inevitable premature death of her only son, and now Chopin saw his own terminal illness as something comical.

He thought of his mother's final days and turned to the gray skies that reflected his bowels and the soup of his ailments. He felt the roar of border life convulsing, and the faces around him disappeared and became merely the sound of their breathing—the short breaths took over people's bodies, their vehicles, the buildings, even the landscape, and the world became an Old West of incomplete breaths—Chopin was unable to hear anything else. He felt himself about to start retching again, but held it—for all he was worth, he held it, and kept walking amid the breathing around him.

Remorse and grief aside, he said to himself, "That was that, and this is now, and I must reclaim the Pleyel."

Chopin looked at his left hand and found he was holding a lottery ticket, then remembered (as if he were experiencing it all over again) running into his favorite street vendor, Don Álvarito, and buying a lottery ticket a block and a half back. He wondered what kind of bill he could've given him, because he didn't have small change in any pocket.

He pulled out the yellow customs papers and quickly fanned through them and put them away.

Chopin began slightly obsessing over a scientist he'd once read about. He didn't recall the scientist's name, but he remembered reading about how this scientist could prove to anyone quite simply that we live in a half world and we are all half beings. That we are all divided in half and it is only an illusion that we've filled out the rest—in this world, the scientist could prove, we are here to strive to fill the other half of ourselves in order to be born as full beings in the next life. Chopin remembered a quote from the scientist, saying, "Most people fail and they keep coming back as half beings. Until, one hopes, they learn and can be born as full beings in a forthcoming life."

He wished he'd read the rest of the article then. At least far enough to find out how he could become a full being himself.

Since the death of his mother, that article had somehow become very present in his mind. It seemed to him a logical explanation of this reality. Physically we are halves, yes—we are born divided in half, yes; our real half is our imperfect half, yes; and, yes, we live out this life trying to fill in our other half, the one that would make us perfect, yes—and our brains, our brains are so powerful they collectively fill in the rest of ourselves so we won't see how gruesome our insides are, yes; so we are always fooling ourselves, yes, yes.

Thinking this way worried him, but more and more the whole scheme of it made sense.

Chopin coughed and again was able to laugh at the cough.

Outside the customs office, by the curb, were two men in nice hats and flashy clothing having a conversation and smoking cigarettes with a police officer. The police officer laughed a laugh like ball bearings in a blender, and one of the sharp-looking men smiled and winked at Chopin.

Chopin thought the men must be musicians in their own right, since their wardrobe resembled that of corrido players.

Chopin gave the winking man a half nod and muttered

something that sounded like *Buenos días* as he walked past them into the customs office.

He took a number upon entering the proper room, and as if he was expected, a worker with poofy auburn hair signaled to him from behind a desk. Chopin looked around to make sure she meant him, then walked up to her. Standing up, the worker asked if he was who he was. He showed her an ID and she said, "Your case has been taken care of" in Spanish.

Chopin struggled to explain it to her—how he'd had to play a show on the American side the previous day, not his first, but hopefully his last. And upon coming back during the thunderstorm, the customs people had confiscated his piano, and now they required him to pay a tax equal to a third of its worth, since it wasn't a Mexican-made piano. A Mexican-made piano—what even is that?

It was a new law, she told him then, to encourage Mexicans to buy Mexican-made products.

Chopin found himself losing his patience and casually mentioned he'd just buried his mother, and now the Mexican government was holding his piano for ransom—what an outrage. He exclaimed that he was a simple artist with the urgency and need to keep making his living, a living more and more denied to him as time went by and that was secretly killing him.

The worker placed her hand on Chopin's shoulder and he stopped talking mid-sentence.

With a droll air, the worker repeated, "Your case has been taken care of."

She grabbed the customs forms from Chopin's hand and tore them up and threw them into the wastebasket.

"I don't understand," he said.

"It's easy. Your piano's been retrieved. They've paid the tariff and some deliverers showed up to take it. Have a nice day. Go play your piano."

Chopin had many questions, so he hesitated before walking away. The lady disappeared into the dim yellow of the cavernous office.

"It's going to be delivered?" he shouted. "By who?"

Outside, Chopin was still wondering how his piano would arrive when he pieced it together: the two sharp-looking men he'd seen making the police officer laugh were suddenly before him, and one of them started to talk. He was friendly, respectful, and not at all threatening to Chopin. Chopin looked directly at him and tried to listen. Across the street was a seafood restaurant called La Piedra y el Pez. As the man talked, Chopin, as if lost in a storm, found harbor in the logo of La Piedra y el Pez—it was an illustration of a tiny fish about to be eaten by a medium fish about to be eaten by a big fish. They looked like different sizes of the same species, painted red and blue, with sharp yellow teeth.

Chopin was inside a dark pickup truck when he snapped out of it. They'd put a luchador mask over his head with the eyes and mouth sewn shut, and were driving along bumpy terrain as Chopin tried to think if he'd agreed to anything—he didn't recall saying a single word to either of the men, but was in this truck riding the terrain of some acne-scarred planet.

He wasn't afraid or alarmed, nor did he feel any kind of way about what was happening, and in the darkness under the mask he thought again about his mother—mostly, about the mirror in his mother's room, the same room in which the disease finally took her. It was a tall and slightly oval mirror, in which you could see your whole body reflected if you stood far enough away.

The morning after the Cruz Roja took his mother, Chopin had sat on her bed and wept for her—wept for the pain she'd suffered, and for the way she'd finally been taken. As he wept, he looked into the mirror. He couldn't remember how, but a white shawl had been placed around it and fluffed so that it looked like a pair of wings. With tears on his face, he laughed. Wings? What? It can't be, he thought. Then, with some shame, he caught his reflection. Chopin noticed how mirrors are a lot like human eyes, and when looking into that mirror he felt the gaze of his dead mother.

He now felt himself lying vertically in a field of tall grass, the sun hot on his face, and he could feel every stem of the grass against his cheeks and forehead—he was climbing down a thick oak tree, when light and dust and a splash of wind like cold, still water dripped down his sweaty hair, and his eyes finally focused, and he came to. There were blurry figures surrounding him. For a few seconds he thought one of the blurry figures was holding a decapitated head for everybody to see, and its face was blue and red just like the fish illustrations at La Piedra y el Pez—but it wasn't a head; those were also the colors of the luchador mask. One of the well-dressed men was holding it up, and turned it inside out for the others to see—there was apple-red blood on the mask. Chopin was handed a golden handkerchief, and a large man with a machine gun and a mustache pantomimed a mouth-wiping gesture to the great pianist.

There was a brief commotion among the men, one of them screaming about how the boss didn't want the pianist harmed in any way, and Chopin felt something wet tickle his left fingers. It was the tongues of two poodles standing on their hind legs and groomed in a very tacky manner, one black, one white. Chopin coughed a loud cough into the golden handkerchief and frightened the poodles. The men stopped arguing and watched him.

Meanwhile, a figure in slacks and a buckled bathrobe and no undershirt approached the dogs. The poodles pranced in his direction. The man had a thick, round face, with a pronounced silver mustache that matched his slightly disheveled hair. Along the left side of his face were clusters of raw boils that'd obviously been scratched and were now caked in a white balm. The boils ran down his neck and into his bathrobe like scuttling baby rats, some flared with yellow pus.

There were movements made and mustached voices were sucked into the pallid atmosphere. Firmly, Chopin's hand, the one not holding the golden handkerchief, was shaken by the man in the bathrobe. Chopin felt his feet walking on the boils of the man's face—he saw the wingspan of a buzzard in the sky, and noticed the castle-like mansion they were approaching. Chopin stopped walking and half stumbled. One of the men carrying a machine gun caught him, and to all of them it appeared Chopin was laughing a madcap laugh. When he pulled the golden handkerchief away from his face, it had on it a thick chunk of what looked like bloodied chewed bubblegum.

Chopin saw that the men around him were no longer wearing their flashy clothing and were now all in black. They'd become medieval sentries, and the man in the bathrobe with the boils was a half-naked king. Everything was music-less and dark—the castle was under some kind of spell. The sound of silent mourning trickled from all around: from the paintings on the wall, the cracked marble statues, the dead plants.

The king was talking to Chopin. The sentries remained silent, and Chopin faintly nodded during his pauses. The king, with droopy potato-sack eyes, gesticulated piano playing in the air.

Chopin did the same, but moved his fingers slower and they turned into the legs of tarantulas.

The king then mentioned the state of Michoacán.

Chopin repeated, "Michoacán?"

"Yes," the king reiterated, "Michoacán."

"No," Chopin said, "I've never been invited to play in Michoacán."

All their faces expressed deep regret over this tragedy.

Chopin looked at the golden handkerchief in his hand

and it finally clicked about the blood. He stuck the handkerchief into his coat pocket, slowly wadding it up into a ball, with slight shame.

He looked into the king's eyes and recognized the boiling red roses of inconsolable sadness and little sleep. He felt, also, a mournful presence guiding them like a spirit through a graveyard—so strong was this sensation that Chopin kept looking around for another person.

They were standing in something like a large ballroom. Chopin looked up at the twenty-foot ceiling with stalactite chandeliers and felt trapped. There was a wall that seemed to be an entire mirror on the other side of the ballroom—Chopin waved his arm and saw it wave all the way over there.

They continued walking through bright corridors with covered windows. He noticed strips of mirrors outlining the walls in every room and hall—to Chopin they felt like eyes winking at him, at first seductively, then like a warning or a secret code telling him to watch his back.

But to Chopin, none of it mattered. He was there. He was following this man through the mansion, and they were being trailed by these goons with guns.

Chopin coughed, this time quietly, with his mouth closed, and swallowed the blood. Using his tongue, and his mouth still closed, he wiped his front teeth.

Everybody stopped walking when they got to a tall, white reinforced-steel door with black trim. To Chopin it looked more like an ascending staircase. He felt they'd finally reached their destination and the static in his head was now harmonizing. The man with the boils opened the infinite pale door and crept inside, alone. All the goons in flashy clothes with machine guns took the opportunity to quickly check their cell phones. One took a selfie next to Chopin.

They were finished by the time the man in the bathrobe crept back out, and he motioned for Chopin and only a single goon to follow him in.

The windowless room had higher ceilings than the rest of the mansion, with strong artificial daylight throughout. There was faint music coming from the far end of the room. Painted on the ceiling was a blue sky and billows of clouds floating all around so that it was perpetually a nice day there in that giant room. Chopin turned to the wall behind him and faced the painted streets of Ancient Greece around the white steel door. He followed the man in the bathrobe toward the faint music—as they got closer Chopin saw a man on a ladder painting a mural: the landscape of Paris.

Then he heard the black keys of the Pleyel and quickly turned around.

The man in the bathrobe was plucking at them—behind him, Chopin saw two men dressed like doctors.

"Wait a minute here," Chopin said out loud.

Nobody heard this.

About five feet to the right of the doctors was a red, pink, and orange exposed canopy bed—it was the biggest bed Chopin had ever seen, and he wondered why he hadn't noticed this as soon as he walked in.

Chopin felt the breathing of the machines. He felt a deep rumble in his chest and dared not to cough again.

On the edge of the canopy bed, Chopin saw an unconscious harp seal dressed in an emerald evening gown. To its left was an elderly woman knitting and humming, and to the left of her were two stoic doctors. Their ankles were chained to snakes that crawled along the floor of the room toward the wall. The rumble Chopin had confused for music came from the various pieces of medical equipment surrounding the doctors, who looked sorrowful about being silent witnesses to this scene.

Chopin stared into the eyes of the doctors, couldn't stand it, and looked immediately away, then made eye contact with the knitting elderly woman.

When he looked back at the open canopy bed, he saw that the figure in the emerald gown was not a harp seal but a hairless young girl. A scalding sense of desert starvation ran through Chopin.

The man in the bathrobe knelt in front of the sleeping young girl, and he seemed to weep quietly as he pressed her emaciated hand to the good side of his face. Chopin saw a revolver dangling from under his bathrobe.

The hairless young girl had no eyebrows and she wore a beret that matched her gown. Her skin was gray and taut. She had her nostrils and arms attached to the droning and fatigued machines. Chopin paid no mind to the two doctors and felt a sweaty hand shaking his right. It was the hand of the young mural painter, whose face he recognized from some glossy magazine page.

Chopin sat on a stool before his Pleyel piano, the piano he'd been playing since he was a boy, and which was his only possession—what remained of his once-privileged upbringing and what his father had often jokingly and prophetically referred to as his sole inheritance.

Chopin didn't notice, but he had started playing its keys—in them were the trees swaying, painted like the trees out west—in them was the pact we've made with the animals and people living in mirrors that are doomed to imitate us—don't forget, animals and mirrors—blankets on the moon and sun and bed, don't forget—stars in lagoons, artificial skies, melting wax and burning wickers, childhood toys, don't forget. Chopin played an improvisation, sweating over the keys, and looked like a melting iceberg—cold, prayerless nights, don't forget, the insects that have bitten us and taken our blood and fragments of our skin—good mothers who have taught us how to read, how to hum before a sunset, knitting scarves and quilts that have kept us warm, don't forget—people in the streets we've bought papers or candy from, window washers, don't forget. Chopin thought he saw the girl in the emerald gown standing on the bed to watch him, the man in the bathrobe sitting along its edge—those dark, lonely rooms in which we've braved both winter and heat, don't forget—don't forget the pain we have felt, what we've been through—everyday things, our chairs, and tables we've shared our meals on, our trembling cars and utensils that helped feed us, don't forget—don't forget the person you've fed, fork, knife, don't forget whose steak you burned, oven and fire—don't forget whom you're denying white blood cells, blood—

don't forget what you're doing to me, lungs, what you're doing to me, dark sky with your big turd clouds—don't forget what you've taken from me and what you will keep taking and with what satisfaction, to what end other than the casket, which can't really be a casket, but a canoe out at sea that we slowly embark in, reminding the sea we once bathed in it and walked its sands—don't forget us, sea, don't forget us, sands— wolves rising early for their prey, don't forget—don't forget the doves we've fed, the sound of horses' hooves, dogs barking at us, don't forget us, dogs—don't forget us, distant yesterdays and impossible tomorrows, whales under moonlight, blood upon clear, green waters, don't forget—sea-dark wine we've consumed, lilies and cherries and shrieks of distant wells where children once drowned, don't forget us while we are still here, while there is still time, desperate-to-be-loved bell tower up high somewhere far off and tragically echoing—fill our lungs again, like when we were young and music still meant something—don't forget whom you once stomped on, dirt.

Chopin played, played, played, when suddenly the painted-sky ceiling cracked in half and lifted to the heavens and let in a macabre whirlwind—the doctors, the elderly woman knitting, the man in the bathrobe, and the girl in the emerald evening gown looked up at a giant bird with plumage like the dusk of dreams, its beak the size of a clipper ship shot down into the room, opened—the girl in the emerald gown unhooked herself from the machines and crawled into the flesh-colored beak. Chopin played-played-played, the man in the bathrobe pulled out the revolver and unloaded it on the bird—the goons ran into the room and machine gun fire cursed-cursed-cursed, Chopin's fingers grew hairy like tarantulas again, the keys of the Pleyel dripped with his sweat as the bird creature flew away with the dying girl—don't forget us, bird—giant bird of the apocalypse, we'll meet again, bird, we'll meet again, frozen lake dreams—dreams—don't forget us, dreams.

Sunrise or sunset—the light of day heaved from his chest as Chopin once again woke up with muddy shoes on his cot. The Pleyel piano was there, in its usual spot by the window. He felt the wad of cash in his coat, pulled it out, and looked at it. Next to his head was the blue-and-red luchador mask with the holes sewn shut, but he didn't touch it. Then he looked at the piano. It was definitely there. He was definitely back in his room off Plaza Bonifacio. He got up, coughed into the toilet in a less violent manner than he'd recently been accustomed to, flushed, and stared at that old Pleyel piano again. Now that it was back, he no longer felt like playing it.

THE 29TH OF APRIL

I am going to tell you a story about your birthday.

It falls on the same day Rosa died. Rosa lived out in *la colonia* they call El Charco, but its real name is Doctores, right outside the city—a border town not too close to the border. Rosa's husband left her and her two boys when the eldest was, I think, five or six, and the younger was three or four. He left them to come work in the States. The plan was that he'd send them money every month, and that he'd come visit as often as he could—this was in the days when it still wasn't too difficult to cross the border. You could even get a driver's license here in Texas if you didn't have any papers. Well, José María—Rosa's husband—never returned to see his boys or his wife, not even once. Nobody ever found out what happened to him, but they say he probably met another woman and didn't look back. And that's how those boys grew up, without a father. They attended school for a while. The older one, his name was Ramiro, but everybody called him El Madonna. You know these boys, they grow up giving nicknames to everybody, and the silliest ones, too. They called Ramiro Madonna like the singer because he had blondish hair and lighter skin than most other kids in the neighborhood. Not anywhere near being actual yellow blond, but there was a clear distinction to warrant the nickname from the other boys. So Madonna was Madonna, and his little, darker-complexioned brother was just Ricky. Madonna was a kid who couldn't control his temper. He was prone to fights in and out of the classroom. He was attracted to hanging around older kids from El Charco, bad influences. Despite all this, Madonna was the son Rosa favored. Not on purpose. I don't believe so. Rosa was never conscious of the way she mistreated little Ricky, I can tell you that much. But it was little Ricky who did well in his studies. Ricky avoided fights and participated in the church early on. He was involved with the kids from El Charco only because of his older brother, this Madonna. Madonna became an active El Charco member when he was very young. When he was around ten years old, I want to say. Hanging around the older boys, probably running favors for them. Witnessing God knows what types of crimes and atrocities. Listening to the kind of music they considered revolutionary—misogynist, violent, lacking real poetry. Madonna grew up this way, and eventually somebody put a gun in his hand. When you're that young and somebody hands you a weapon, you start believing in its sick reality. So Madonna played with guns. He stopped attending school and Rosa never objected. Madonna would bring her money almost on a daily basis, at first stolen, or offerings from the kids begging for alms in the street. This is how Rosa stopped cutting hair for a living. When the boys got older, and Madonna grew to be the leader of El Charco, Rosa already had that little dress shop by the Avenida Lázaro Cárdenas. You probably never got a chance to go, but I took my son's daughter Gabrielita there a few times to be measured for a dress. Rosa adored her little business. She turned a silent eye to the reality of her sons and ran her dress shop with pride and humility. It was Rosa's disposition to be soft-spoken. The only one person she seemed to have the ability to reproach was Ricky. Little Ricky was the boy who continued with his studies. That boy, I remember his face, *moreno* like my father. And like the man I married. Of the two boys, I remember Ricky better. He was a good boy. Madonna kept him very close. Except on those early runs, when Madonna was only a hanger-on to the bigger kids, he always took Ricky along. He'd be the one to drop off Ricky at school and pick him up in the middle of the day. The place of refuge outside their home for these boys was a house that had once been Doña Carmelita's. Nobody remembers her now, but after she passed away there was nobody to claim that house of hers. A few years later the El Charco boys took it over. Before all the drug business came along, that's where they ran their dogfights, and sometimes out-of-towners would show up with *gallos* and they'd hold cockfights there, too. And the police—no, there's no such thing as the police, we end up learning. We read things or see something in the news of the goings-on in another country and we think, How could anybody live like that—we forget that the same things are happening around us, or with us, up and down the border. The dogfights were constant. It's how things changed with Madonna. There were no more robberies in the neighborhood. If Madonna heard of anybody who robbed, he was the first to do something about it. Gambling and the dogfights were how the money was made—again, before the drugs came in. Every night, still, they'd get home to have dinner with Rosa, and Ricky would stay to do his schoolwork. Madonna was the one who went off to do business on his own in the night. I don't want to say the brothers grew distant, because I don't believe this was the case. But they were growing. Changing. In their own way, with what their surroundings allowed. Madonna got deeper into the world of gangs and all that darkness. I didn't find out about the drugs until everybody was already surrounded by them—without even knowing it. With the people of my generation it was different, especially how we grew up, on the rancho, and in southern Mexico. It started with hearing about somebody's boy getting shot. Then somebody's husband disappearing. Then more and more frequent gunshots in the night, and the confusion that comes with them, especially in those first few seconds, that first minute, actually, of silence after gunshots. You brace yourself for what that silence will bring. One time I ran into Madonna at the little *deposito* that was Don Chuy's. I had my brother coming to visit me and wanted to make some *mole* the way we had when we were young. I walked into Don Chuy's and there was Madonna, buying a *kilo de tortillas*. He was wearing one of those sleeveless shirts with a bandanna over his head like you see kids in the movies wearing, and as I was walking out he held the door open for me and he smiled. That smile, I remember, gave me such a feeling. I felt sad for the boy, though at the time I knew only rumors of his dealings. There was something in that smile, I now know, that warned of something bigger, almost like a warning about all of the border—that what was going on in the neighborhood was what was going on in the entire *frontera*, that this was what was happening to all of our children when they left us for the United States or the world of guns in our streets. I walked away wanting to hug the boy, I don't know why, as if he were my own son. I thought about my own sons and felt relief that they were already grown men with beautiful families of their own. And I thought about Rosa and thought to visit her at the dress shop. I didn't know it then, but little Ricky had been with a girl and they were expecting a child together. The girl was living with Rosa during the time Ricky was nowhere to be found. Rosa had gotten mean with Ricky when the girl came to their doorstep after being kicked out by her family. I never understood that about some families. If my daughter came to me scared to death and with child in that manner, how could I kick her out? So Rosa took her in and Ricky fell into El Charco. Probably staying at Doña Carmelita's old house on Calle Enrique Bustamante. The boys no longer ran dogfights or cockfights there. It was where they kept the drugs that passed through. The guns the boys carried, I noticed, changed to bigger guns. The deadlier weapons they call *ma-tralletas* or *cuerno de chivos*. More and more deaths were reported in the papers. The bodies of dead men and dead boys kept being found, and of women, too, but rarely, not like in other places. Not yet. Bigger gangs from the South were wanting to move in and were not afraid to take things by force. Police officers came by and did the bare minimum. A few times we even saw some reporters asking questions everybody was afraid to answer. But the reporters stopped coming when we started finding them dead. The gangs began to threaten anyone who reported on their activities. One of the popular female reporters was assaulted, too, and then murdered, along with her children, after she ran a story about a shooting in the market. Those big gangs made the small gangs like El Charco accomplices—the ones who refused were murdered. Drugs were sold openly in the middle of the day. I remember looking out my window at this young man with bad skin whom people would approach all day long. One time I got tired of it and called the police. When the police came by, I saw them talk to the young man selling drugs, and they carried on and on in pleasant conversation, as if old friends. Even laughing. Then the police drove away and the young man kept that post in front of my house for a long time. That's when my little place started being harassed. My petunias and *floresitas* that I had kept for years started being uprooted. Strangers would jump my little fence and trample all over my patch of grass until everything stopped growing and I started becoming miserable, living all by myself. My husband had been dead many years already, but I started talking to him in the evenings as I had my *cafésito* at our little kitchen table. I'd yell at him, "*Me dejaste, viejo*; you left me, *descarado*." Then I'd beg him to stay by my side, that growing up all alone is something nobody deserves. Or I'd tell him about our sons and how well they were doing, how proud we both should be. Always I'd say how much I missed him. And how the neighborhood is not what it was. My days became dizzy this way. I became lost in the abyss of what my life was becoming. I would leave the house only to go to the *mercado* and cash the little allowance my sons sent me, and in the evenings I'd have coffee with my dead husband, *que en paz descanse*. On one of those evenings, looking into the street, I encountered the wagon that picked up our trash, passing by. It was one of those wagons with a man holding the reins and a whip, and pulled by a skinny horse wearing blinders. But this man had his little girl and his little boy sitting by him. They were dressed in dirty clothes. The man stopped the wagon in front of the house and he got off to grab my trash can and emptied it into the back of the open wagon. He already had a big pile accumulated, I noticed, when I looked at all their faces. The three of them—their faces were drawn blank, hauling all that trash. They had no expression to them. The man yanked at the reins on that poor horse, and as they pulled away I was able to do something I hadn't been able to bring myself to do before. I cried. I don't remember ever crying so much. Searching and searching through my mind, as tears kept rolling down my face, I couldn't think of any reason for them. I went through everything that saddened me, the death of my mother, living so far away from my sons, not being able to see my granddaughters grow up, my dead husband. Then I pinched my own skin, twisting it hard, not knowing why either. I laughed and thought, *Me estoy volviendo loca*, and laughed even more. Time passed, because the next thing I remember was waking up and it was the middle of the night. I got myself together and took a long shower. Afterward I fell back asleep, and when I awoke the next morning, in a voice that was almost not my own, I said to myself, "I'm going to visit Rosa at her dress shop today." I brewed some coffee and poured it into a thermos and bought some fresh pan dulce from Don Chuy. I walked the four and a half blocks to her dress shop, and when I got there Rosa was watching her morning shows on a little color television she kept behind the counter. The inside of the shop was decorated like an altar. There were photographs all over the walls, some of them framed and others just carefully taped up, with ribbons as borders around them. There were little bells from past weddings and funerals, and tiny ceramic infants from old baptisms, too. On the walls there were no pictures of her husband, José María. Plenty of pictures of Madonna and Ricky; you could see them grow up being there merely ten minutes and looking around. I don't remember what we talked about that time. We probably just had the pan dulce and café and watched her little color television. Either that week or shortly after that, a car exploded two blocks down the street from me, in the opposite direction from

Rosa's shop. In plain day, around noon or one in the afternoon. I was listening to my favorite program on the radio when it happened, and I didn't have to turn it down to know it had been real. I walked outside and opened my little gate. I saw young boys in shorts running down the street toward the thick black smoke, and some of the younger ones were laughing and dancing as if a fire like this were a cause for celebration. I heard some people yelling, and as I got closer to the scene I could feel the intensity of that fire. Some of the younger mothers kept yelling for the firemen. There were no sirens. I saw young women pull out hoses from a few of the houses and they sprayed the burning car, which only seemed to make the smell worse. Moments later a man in a tiny truck stepped out carrying a silver extinguisher and sprayed that stuff all over the fire until the fire was out and you'd think it had snowed on this car in our neighborhood in the middle of the incredible heat of that year. An hour or so later the firemen showed up and did nothing. They measured things on the ground around the car, sure. Luckily nobody was hurt, and other than the car, nothing was destroyed. When the neighborhood people talked, nobody seemed to know where the car had come from. Nobody saw who drove it or who parked it in that spot. It was almost like a senseless prank. By then everything really was gray. Little Ricky had gone back to live with Rosa, and had even married the girl, who was now very pregnant. He continued with his studies and was the first in his family to graduate from secondary school. What you call high school here. Madonna climbed life differently from his brother. He did a lot more running around, not just in the neighborhood. Sometimes he was gone for days. Madonna stopped having dinner every night with Rosa and the family. He started to dress differently, too, wearing silk shirts and nice boots and sombreros. Madonna never hesitated to give Rosa money or take his brother along to attend to neighborhood business now and then. This is how Ricky was able to make money, too, while they waited for his baby boy to be born—in the drug business. The drug business took over everything. The big gangs approached the little gangs like benefactors wearing fine cologne, offering them money and drugs to work for them, and threatening the ones who saw a trap or simply refused. Madonna still ran Doña Carmelita's house with the El Charco boys, but now it was the bigger gang that owned it. Overnight, the bigger gangs owned everything, including people's fears. I had noticed Rosa was losing weight. I didn't think anything of it. The thought that she could be sick didn't even cross my mind. My visits to her shop became habitual. I'd go see Rosa some mornings—never on any particular day. Only on days I would feel it, I would say maybe two or three times a week. As my visits grew, I'd always test the waters with Rosa. I'd ask her discreetly about her boys, how they were doing, et cetera. Rosa would simply dab at my questions. She'd say her boys were well. How well Ricky was doing in school. How well *los negocios* of Madonna were going. Of course, she didn't call him Madonna, but by his name, Ramiro. And she'd refer to what Ramiro did as his *negocios*. His business. One of those days she invited me to

Mass with her and Adriana, Ricky's wife. Ricky and Madonna rarely attended Mass. Ricky did sometimes. I remember him accompanying us; he was always smiling and polite to me, and during Mass he knew all the prayers and orations from his boyhood days of attending. I don't know if it restored my faith, but I enjoyed Mass, and, later, getting to know the fathers. Padre Aldama, Padre German, *el joven* Padrecito Vicente. I got to know some of the other women in the congregation, but never well. We'd never invite one another into our lives. Even still, with Rosa it was always difficult talking. The times I mentioned my husband in passing, Rosa responded only with Catholic gestures, like crossing herself, or assuring me that my husband was now in God's hands. Then all at once everything escalated. A politician was murdered, along with his family and drivers and maids and guards, in his own home at the capital. Soldiers started casually patrolling the streets with expressionless faces, like the kids I'd seen with their father on the wagon. Gunshots were heard daily, either from a distance, a long distance, like the death of a star, or sometimes shockingly close. There would be minor mentions of gun battle in the papers. I'd look out my window and know the reporters weren't doing their jobs. Everything was being downplayed. The politicians assured us the violence was mostly exaggerated and that in reality it wasn't that bad. As things got worse, we read less about it; the local news programs focused on labor strikes and sewage problems in the developing areas outside town. Early one morning, as I was sweeping my porch, I heard screaming from one of the young mothers a few houses down. I thought at first that she'd been assaulted, that she'd been hurt. This young mother, it turned out, wasn't a mother yet. It was Esencia, a young wife fairly new to the neighborhood. She was a little over seven months pregnant. I didn't know what she was doing, but as she screamed people huddled around her, men and women and children, some of them weeping, but all of them trying to console Esencia. Then, using her fists, she started pounding her pregnant belly. Pounding it with rage, tears in her eyes. It left me dumbstruck. The people around her tried to restrain her, and she kicked the air and screamed for them to let her go. Finally they let Esencia go and she dropped, coiled herself into a little ball by the lamppost until somebody brought her water and she calmed down. Her husband had been found dead in an abandoned vehicle by the Rio Bravo. He was one of the El Charco boys, around the same age as Madonna. They'd been married for almost a year. There was an investigation, but his death didn't appear in the newspaper, not even an obituary. A few days after that, I learned about Rosa being sick. And from the neighborhood news I learned that Madonna had been arrested for his involvement in something or other. The rumors were that he and the now-dead young husband had left the neighborhood together and had never come back. Rosa, in passing, one visit, told me—as if she were picking a nice flower—that she thought she had breast cancer. I asked if she'd seen a doctor and she said no. I asked if there was a tumor, and when she said yes, I demanded that she show me. When she refused, I knew just the person to call and scheduled an appointment with Dr. Ruiz de Zoa Zoa. She said she didn't have the money and I said, "*Al infierno con el dinero*, Rosa," and had to really drag her over there myself. I learned that Rosa's cancer was very accelerated and that she'd actually known about it for a long time. When she'd discovered it, the cancer would have still been easily treatable, but Rosa had refused any kind of treatment, out of I don't know what. She hadn't even told any of her family. When she said I was the only person she'd told, just as easily and mysteriously to me as before, I'd started to cry, asking Rosa, "Why, Rosa—why did you do this to yourself?" I squeezed her hands as I pleaded with her, and we held each other and cried. Then I got angry at Rosa and called her selfish and inconsiderate. That's how fate had it, because I ended up storming out of there and off to my own house, cursing Rosa the whole way. I heard gunshots a few blocks out and the soldiers in their trucks sped by. I heard televisions from other houses, and the *elotero* pushing his cart rang his bell. In my little home I lit some candles. I sat in my kitchen and waited for the sun to go down. Inevitably, time passed and Rosa got worse. Adriana, Ricky's wife, had already given birth, and had been apprenticing with Rosa at the dress shop. Slowly, she started taking it over, and Rosa got to spend more time at home. That's where I'd go visit her at this point. There were some weeks when things were calm, and other weeks when you heard of more killings and about the drugs, which never stopped being sold. Again, it happened fast, and everything showed itself as it really was.

Neighborhood boys parading around with guns became a normal thing, and you hardly ever saw the soldiers anymore. If you did, you knew it was merely a formality. I'd go to Rosa's home, and as Rosa got sicker I finished her chores, so she could rest in bed. Adriana tended the shop, and I'd get people to visit Rosa. A couple of the priests came by, and Padre German made it a habit to visit on Thursday afternoons, sometimes also on Mondays. I went through a long period without hearing about Madonna. Nobody would even mention his real name. I'd want to ask Rosa about him sometimes, even just about the boys' upbringing, but I never dared. After secondary school, Ricky never followed up with his studies—and after Madonna's arrest and disappearance, I'm afraid it was Ricky who became involved in all that even more. By then everybody around knew about Rosa being sick. Neighborhood people were kind to her, offering to help Rosa around the house. Dr. Ruiz de Zoa Zoa had moved to the South after the practice next to his was robbed by armed men. But he didn't abandon us; he referred us to a trusted colleague of his, with roots here on the border. On the day I heard Ricky had been abducted, I went over to Rosa's. Not with the plan of staying there overnight—of course not. But I felt the need to protect her. I'll never forget how Rosa looked during those last weeks. She was emaciated, all the color taken from her skin: the sweet woman was pallid. In the middle of the night a few days later, Rosa's dress shop was burned down, shot with bullets, and all the nice dresses Rosa had made, all the fabric she had acquired, was scattered over Avenida Lázaro Cárdenas. I didn't tell Rosa. I couldn't. I'm sure she heard, but not from me. Rosa hardly spoke as her life drifted away. Adriana packed up her things and with her son went to live in Tampico at her sister's. And Ricky—nobody heard about Ricky again. He was never reported as arrested, and a body was never found. Ricky just vanished, like his father. Left no room to mourn his loss. I would cook meals and take care of matters in my own home; when I finished, I'd walk over to Rosa's and try to tidy up her home, too. Rosa would sometimes do simple things herself, but I'd always urge her not to, tell her that she had me for those things, to which she never replied. It could get hot in Rosa's home. I thought things were bad in my place, but Rosa's was much worse. She didn't even have ceiling fans, and a *tortilleria* had opened right behind her place, so we felt the heat of the machines. I couldn't stand it. But at the same time, I had to. I was no longer my own person. I hardly recognized the people in the neighborhood, and the children seemed to have vanished, too. Don Chuy had passed away, same as his wife, Violeta. I no longer talked to my dead husband. I had even given up drinking coffee in the evenings and left it only as part of my morning routine. Maybe I became a little like Rosa. I felt, or thought I felt, how much sadness there was in everything, and instead of letting it provoke more negative thoughts, I let it numb me. Suspicious vehicles passed by, and I saw young girls getting picked up by older men all the time. And in the news, still nothing. With all that, my son Sebastian had become a good communicator with me. He began calling more often, and eventually, as we talked about our changing lives, he asked me to come live with him up here in Falfurrias, with his wife and daughters. I didn't want to at first. I thought that at my age a big change like moving from one country to another would be too much. I learned to laugh at the stubbornness of that statement. To everyone's surprise, it was reported in the papers that Madonna had been found dead. Stabbed numerous times all over his body. He had escaped from prison with the aid of some of the guards and had started other dealings in another state. They found him dead in the city of China, that desolate nowhere-town between here and Monterrey. In the paper they referred to him as Madonna, and said he was from our neighborhood, Doctores, and was the once leader of the gang El Charco. They had a picture of him looking like a dapper young man, his blondish hair slicked back. I kept that article on my kitchen table for a long time, with that picture facing up, his hazel eyes looking right at me, his face clean-shaven. It couldn't be real, but there he was, and never did I say anything to Rosa. On almost every wall of Rosa's house, her sons' photos hung, but we didn't speak of them. Padre German and I arranged for Rosa to be moved to a better place, where there would be nurses attending to her at all times. That's where Rosa died. Her body was cremated and we held a little service and vigil in the church for her. I didn't recognize any of the few people there. The night of her service was particularly gunshot-heavy, and I still had Rosa's house keys with me. I wondered what would happen to her home now. I heard cars screeching past, blocks away, and machine gun blasts, and loud noises from the streets that in my memory are now so narrow, more like corridors. I sat in Rosa's kitchen that evening. I had her radio playing low when the phone rang. Its ring was foreign to me, and I remembered where the phone was, in the living room, and I answered, "*Bueno?*" It was a woman on the other end, who presented herself as a reporter calling from Mexico City. I was shaking, more from fear than anything else, as I remembered stories of drug addicts pretending to be relatives asking for ransom, saying they needed money because they were being held captive. But the reporter assured me she was who she said she was, and that she was working on a piece about the violence along the border. That she'd been randomly dialing listed numbers of people in neighborhoods where she'd heard the violence was beyond control. As she talked, I kept wanting to interrupt, wanting to say, *Yes, it's true,* señorita, *listen to what's going on here in this moment; listen to those bullets, to those lost neighborhood boys shooting one another.* She asked if I felt there was a news blackout here, and explained to me what a news blackout was—when there is actual news going on but it is not being reported. She asked if, in my opinion, politicians' assurances to the public were true, and I told her no, that things were terrible, and I thought this woman must've been sent to me from high above. That she was here to save me and to spread the truth. We talked for a while and made a phone appointment for the following day at the same time. But I knew, after I hung up, that I'd be taking my son's offer and leaving. I felt my life there was over. I've thought many times since about that nice reporter, who came to me at the right time. Because of her, I finally decided it was time to leave. I guess I needed a sign, a stranger's voice to nudge me on. I was finally finished on that day, April twenty-ninth. I have the date here, inside this locket I wear, with Rosa's picture, you see. This day means a lot to me, and that's why I carry the reminder around my neck. And you say it's also your birthday, too, so happy birthday. May you have many, many more.

ZAPATA FOOTS THE BILL

At a shop called La Boutique off Monk Street and Breakfast Avenue, where businesses rarely lasted more than half a year's lease, the muralist Eduardo Salamanca bought a dark brown shirt with an airbrushed image of the revolutionary Zapata. He walked out wearing it, with his old shirt in a plastic bag.

Commissioned to paint a mural that required storyboarding, Salamanca wondered how to go about illustrating the mythical *Book of the Face*. This idea had started out facetiously, but then he saw there was some meaning to a thick book being handed to you, filled with words detailing, in simple yet erudite sentences, your own face. Eduardo Salamanca sat under the awning of Cosma's taco stand downtown, thinking of the binding style a book like this would have and how he'd paint it, and shooed away grackles.

He used the bathroom at a Chevron station, and in the

mirror he admired, beneath his own shaved face, the determination and blue eternity in Zapata's defiant expression on his shirt.

A few blocks later he arrived at the civic center and stared at the wall he was to paint—it was brown, like the rest of the building. Salamanca tried to focus to the point of thinking nothing, then an idea galloped toward him, dismounted, and asked him: At what point does a wall become a mural? *When an image is imposed upon it.* And at what point is a mural a wall again? *When the image is vanquished, by time or by humans.* It was at this point that Eduardo Salamanca's vision of the *Book of the Face* turned into a vision of the wall—he realized how, in the *Book of the Face*, your own face is created not word by word, but with clay, and stone by stone.

Salamanca felt he had to start the mural not by storyboarding with pad and paper, but with bricks and mortar.

The day was cool, with thick chemtrails cutting the sky.

Salamanca removed the Zapata shirt and put on the old one he'd left the house in. For no real reason, he hung the Zapata shirt on a bolt protruding from the brown civic center wall. He stood twenty feet away from it and stared at Zapata, who looked as stoic as ever.

Then, as if it were a challenge, Salamanca lifted a heavy stone from the ground, threw it, and it landed just inches from Zapata's boots. Zapata's eyes moved to the stone, then stared back at Salamanca.

From his vest pocket, Zapata pulled out a raw chicken leg and tossed it up toward the scaly sky. A winged javelina flew down from the northeast, caught it in its jaws, and tore it apart. Clouds swarmed in, turned webbed, then porous like an ant colony. The winged javelina flew into one of the ant holes and disappeared.

Eduardo Salamanca found himself in a land where the entire world was reflected in mirages—the desert. Twenty feet away from him, Zapata bent down, picked up the heavy stone at his feet. Zapata admired the stone as if it were a skull or a tiny seed, designed to create the mythical thousand forests—then, effortlessly, he flung the stone toward the north. The stone elongated in midair, and by the time it hit the ground it had turned ultraviolet, red, orange, then into a dark green snake that slithered away but didn't seem to move. To Eduardo Salamanca, the snake's head and tail were merely stretching in opposite directions, until both became part of the land and the horizon.

In the meantime, Salamanca had many questions for Zapata. For instance: Has the prophecy been postponed? And: Do we need to start recording and broadcasting silence?

Salamanca and Zapata both cautiously approached the eternal snake that'd manifested from the stone. Slime oozed from it. Zapata reached for his pistol, emptied the chambers into his fist, and threw the bullets at a rock that pierced the ground in the direction of the head of the snake. The earth around them split open, and Zapata, along with Salamanca, found himself surrounded by giant boulders and walking through the lowest point of a valley, far from the sun, surrounded by cyclones of darkness and mysterious, dark red hares, who were hopping and chewing on stones. As it got brighter, the Valley deflated and Salamanca noticed that the hares were not chewing on the stones, but polishing them with their faces. The land flattened out, the hares vanished, and Zapata signaled to Salamanca to follow him.

Walking along, Salamanca and Zapata quietly approached six men on horseback wearing gas masks, with machetes strapped to their backs and pistols holstered at their hips. The six of them saluted Zapata. Through an encroaching yellow fog, hoofbeats were heard, then two horses were seen. Zapata and Salamanca mounted these horses and rode with the men. The yellow fog was so thick that Salamanca couldn't see even the head of his horse as they rode. The fog turned achromatic and the world was dark and gray like a dull blade. All eight horses stopped and lined up side by side, and it became apparent to Salamanca that they were at the edge of a precipice, looking down upon a long, flat land-scape, and a colossal structure that ran from the snake's head to the snake's tail, as far as the eye could see. There were people, shackled and chained, facing the structure—the wall—watching as other, unchained people carried bricks and pushed wheelbarrows filled with mortar. The chained people were dressed in rags, whereas the builders were stark naked. Salamanca looked up at the masked riders, and won-dered if they were overseeing and enslaving these people—if Zapata and he had become complicit in this madness.

Salamanca's horse must have slipped, because as it trot-ted along the edge of the valley with the others, it tumbled down the embankment toward the forced laborers and the monumental wall. Salamanca picked himself up, un-harmed, horrified at this level of exposure—he expected some kind of military to pounce on him at any moment. Scared, he ran between the chained people and the naked workers. He looked around for Zapata or the masked men, and, perhaps foolishly, expected a dramatic rescue from them at any moment.

It became apparent that nobody was coming for Sala-manca, neither to arrest nor to rescue him. After walking for miles, for what seemed like days, all he'd seen were hun-dreds of people in rags chained to the ground, and the naked workers building the wall. Salamanca eventually forgot all about Zapata and the stone and the snake. He started to really pay attention to the construction of this colossal wall. The process was unclear but hypnotic to him—he could see the naked builders working on the structure, but how the bricks were stacked all the way to the insurmountable top was a mystery. Soon Salamanca began to have his own ideas about the construction of the wall. He found a spot between two nearly naked people, shackled at their waists and ankles. Salamanca reached for a shackle chained to a stone, and with his own hands clamped it around his neck. He sat on the sandy ground to watch the construction of the wall.

Time passed. It was impossible to tell how much time, because the light came from a mysterious sun that never set. Salamanca's beard was down to his third rib and his clothes had turned to rags. Funny, but Salamanca still got a kick out of watching the naked people building this wall, expecting that at any moment it would be finished.

Long ago, one of his neighbors had torn off her clothes and started participating in the construction, very dully and very slowly. Long after that, the other neighbor had followed. Salamanca got to the point where he thought about nothing, dreamed about nothing except the construction of this wall.

One day, he remembered his previous life—his life as a muralist. On an impulse, he removed the shackle from around his neck and got up. He jogged clumsily through the chained people, the naked workers—then toward the darkness over the embankment. He crawled out of the valley into a wooded area, and after working through tall grass and tree branches, he found a clearing. There was a patch of bright green grass, where Salamanca stopped to catch his breath and decide what to do.

Flies buzzed, the air turned rank and acrid. Salamanca saw the horses and all six mysterious riders lying on the ground just in front of him. As he got closer he noted that the riders had their masks off. He looked for Zapata among the bodies, but he was missing—however, there was his seventh horse, which had been shot.

Salamanca wanted no part of this death scene; he turned and ran away into the dense forest. He thought, The night. Could this really be true? A man like me, blessed to see the nighttime once again?

He found a spot on the ground as good as any other and fell asleep to silence, interrupted only by the occasional howl and creaturely croak. Come dawn, something slithered under his body and Salamanca awoke with a start, immediately picked a direction, and ran. He heard a click, stopped, turned to face a man pointing a pistol at him. The bearded Salamanca, in his ragged clothes, easily recognized the bearded Zapata, still wearing his uniform.

Zapata put the pistol away; both men laughed and rejoiced.

"Those riders that found us were spies for the other side," Zapata exclaimed.

Both of them agreed: screw this conflict, screw this war. They decided to take a break. Zapata found a raft by the river and they both went fishing for mackerel while whistling and singing old tunes. There was an orchard by the bend, where they picked a whole satchel, put up a stand by the road with a sign that said FRESH APPLES, and after a few days of nobody passing by, Salamanca and Zapata accepted their fates. They kicked over the stand and said, "Screw this, too," and went back to their conflict, back to their war.

Inevitably, the subject of ghosts came up, and they argued. To Salamanca, the representation of a ghost as a floating sheet was outdated—perhaps a cheap visual gimmick carried over from the early days of trick photography. For Zapata, the floating sheet represented something deeper than the hokey visual it suggested. "Sure," he said, "there is clearly a person underneath the sheet, and that is laughable. However, when we die we bid farewell not only to this world but also to our flesh, bones, and blood—yet our spiritual fabric continues. So if we're leaving all this behind, and our souls, being this spiritual fabric, come back to haunt, that's what we'd be. A people of floating sheets."

By the time Salamanca and Zapata finished their argument, they'd reached the gate at the far end of the wall. The workers were long gone and there wasn't a tree for miles. Zapata flicked the latch, pushed the gate open. Both of them crossed through to the other side and carefully closed the gate behind them.

This was the story the muralist Eduardo Salamanca tried to tell in the mural along the civic center wall, using an amalgam of styles taken from Pieter Brueghel, the Elder; Remedios Varo; and lowrider truck art. The public accepted it indifferently. Nobody ever got it, and Salamanca never bothered explaining the story using words.

NOSTRADAMUS BABY

The day came when we had trouble hearing, and Denorah and I got excited, for we'd have more wax to add to our Nostradamus baby. Denorah poured the warmed hydrogen peroxide into my ears, then I did the same for her.

We gave each other time to let it tingle and foam, to shift the wax we both felt squishing inside our heads. Less than an hour later we balled together our extracted wax to form a marble almost a quarter inch in diameter. Denorah and I held hands, delighted that our bodies had created this little miracle. We walked up to our Nostradamus baby, which was resting on the living room table. We didn't always have our child out, but it was that time of year, finally, when we could walk right up to our baby and add another bit of wax. Denorah chose to add it, this time, to the spot just below the head, completing the neck that connected to the oblong body.

As we stood there embracing, we looked down upon our

evolving creation, knowing secretly that if we weren't to have children, then at least we could have our Nostradamus baby to keep us company and to bring us warmth in our future graying years.

From our door came a knock, then clattering footsteps: it was Andi, Denorah's older sister, and in a pumpkin-carved voice she exclaimed, "Aha! I timed it right." She held a thermos in her hand and wore bundles of clothes that reeked of various types of smoke: Nag Champa, cigarettes, smog, and pot. She rummaged in the kitchen and emerged with two cups, for us, of what I took to be this tea she constantly sipped from her thermos's maroon lid.

"You know what I did?" she said. "I marked it down last year. Because, actually, I had marked it down the year before that, too. The time you put out this thing. This project, this little creature of y'all's. I'm sorry, okay, I'll respect your baby here. Your child."

Andi got up close to our Nostradamus baby, almost even touching its nose, and said, "Hi, baby. It's me, your tía. That's right, baby, I live just down the block, you can't miss me. I love your mom and dad here forever." She sat back down, and, as if our Nostradamus baby could no longer hear us, continued: "Look, I'm gonna say something you're going to hate to hear. But somebody needs to say it: There are children, not very far from here, who have been separated from their parents and live in cages. I know, that sucks, right? You are wondering, Why did Andi have to say this? Everyone knows this is happening. What good does it do her"—she pointed to herself here—"to spell it out and spoil our fun? So while you're cozy here this winter, adding nasty earwax to your little creature, remember that."

Andi walked out and left the three of us alone again, as a family.

The next day was when I'd agreed to meet up with someone Andi had found who needed to get a spy narrative off the ground. I was worn out by spy narratives but had agreed because it couldn't hurt to make a few extra dollars. So here I was, continuing my streak of unpleasant encounters with Andi. I wondered if thinking this way was helping to create these tense situations with her, so I consciously tried to manifest positive feelings within myself, at least for the moment.

The man was middle-aged, wore a Members Only jacket, and, in a booth at Settler's Coffee, he recounted his spy narrative detail by detail as Andi sat at the counter on her own. Spy narratives were among the most demanding to listen to, because I had to appear to be at the edge of my seat the entire time, when in reality it was the same hoopla narrative recycled from old movies. I'd learned that beginner writers had a strange affinity for protagonists with one wooden leg, and this man was no exception.

Afterward, as we talked together, Andi asked, "Jesus, what do you think it is these people want? To be famous? Do they actually think you'd want to write the story they have in their head, just because you're a published writer? Don't they know you have your own ideas?"

As Andi handed me my cut of the money, I said, "They

probably just want somebody to listen to their story. I'm sure they've worn their families out by now."

"They'd be better suited going to therapy. It probably costs the same. But hey. It helps us. I know you complain that these people don't read your books and don't really care about your career. Bet you never thought that would happen, huh? That as soon as you became a published author, you'd get kinda reversed. And people would want to tell you *their* story instead of reading yours—even pay you good money to listen, way more than the cost of your book. You are lucky, friend. People will talk your ear off and waste your time for absolutely nothing."

I thanked Andi once again for spotting a market and bringing me on. She threw me the peace sign and crossed the street in the opposite way from me.

Home early from her vintage shop, Denorah was three hours into boiling the mushroom stock. We shared a small glazed ham with potatoes for dinner, and when the stock was finished we drank some out of mugs and saved the rest. We came to the conclusion that neither of us had any more wax buildup from our ears to give as offerings to our Nostradamus baby this season. Though we had cherished those moments, the time had come to put our Nostradamus baby away in the tiny box that served as our child's home.

Before my next appointment downtown at Marl's Bakery, I'd calculated my finances for the quarter, and was surprised that I'd saved more than enough money for taxes, all thanks to these little side gigs Andi had hooked up. She had me meeting up to five people a week now to listen to their ideas for books they hoped to one day finish. Often these aspiring writers had a series of books in mind, and this man I was about to meet—Schroeder—had had one in the works for a few years now. Schroeder had actually been one of our first clients. He'd placed an ad in the *Voice* for a ghostwriter and Andi had replied to it. As a joke, she'd proposed this idea to Denorah, and though Denorah had shot her down, she'd joked to me that it was something I'd probably be good at. I had agreed, on the sole condition that I'd never have to read anyone's pages, and Andi told me not to worry.

Schroeder had a series he was working on titled *The World War $$ Chronicles*. His narrative was about World War $$—the final war—and how it had been instigated in 1876 by a bet between chemical-snuffing industrialists. The first book chronicled the late nineteenth century and ended in 1901; the second picked up just a few years before that and ended with World War II. Neither had been drafted; only copious notes had been written by Schroeder. Book three began with the end of the Vietnam War and would lead up to World War $$. Because his books would have such a large cast of characters who came and went, and because Schroeder had not yet written a page, he was still busy mapping out what would happen in the third book. I'd listen to Schroeder talk about his characters and, in our allotted time, would work through their complications in a manner that also propelled the narrative and passage of time.

He couldn't begin to write even the first sentence of the

series, however, until he knew every plot point and detail and had jotted them down. Schroeder was a meticulous note-taker, and he'd filled four five-subject notebooks with notes about his saga. In the beginning I met with Schroeder for only an hour every few weeks, but as we kept fleshing out his narrative, complexities arose that couldn't be ignored; now we were up to two three-hour meetings a week at Marl's Bakery, where the baristas were probably very sick of us.

When I showed up, I found Andi sitting at a table and no Schroeder around. "Have you heard?" Andi said to me in a whisper. "Something escalated with this one country and now everyone is talking of a new war happening. You know how Schroeder is: he decided to stay home and watch the news. He paid us for the time, though, as the contract I negotiated stipulates." She handed me an envelope with my share of the cash.

Feeling an intense rush of freedom, I ordered a six-dollar coffee, and had it in a for-here cup. Andi always seemed fascinated by my personal life as an author and had a habit of probing into my works in progress. One time I'd asked Denorah if she thought her sister had an unhealthy obsession with both of us somehow making it big, and she replied merely by saying her sister was a schemer; this is what she had become as an adult, she explained, how she survived: by figuring out little schemes to make a few extra dollars.

Andi was scrolling through her phone for updates on this possible new war when she suddenly put it away and said, "You're an immigrant, right? Or, no, what do they call you? A war refugee—that's right. Maybe that's the book you should write next, from the perspective of your life as a refugee of war."

"I oughta, right? There won't be a dry eye in all of Brooklyn—"

"You'll sell it for a ton of cash and get loads of attention, no doubt."

"That's possible. But even if I *do* somehow write it, the money wouldn't be worth it."

"But it probably *will* be worth it. You just need to write one of those stories where nothing big happens, but a lot of small, sad things do happen. Things that you overcame and all that."

"There's already a lot of writers out there doing that. I don't need to be adding to it."

"But then you'll get a chance to reach readers with the story of your triumph. They'll turn your book into a movie. Maybe you can even make a complete living as a full-time writer. You won't have to meet with people like Schroeder for extra money. I mean, I certainly don't mind taking a cut, and I'm one to talk . . ."

"That's not storytelling to me, though. Not what storytelling is about."

"What does that even mean? Just write your story from where it begins to how you ended up here. You can even make some of it up. What do you call it? Fictionalizing? And give it some super-artsy title that also makes you think. I can see everyone leaving the theater crying after reading this."

I considered these things Andi was saying, and for a moment looked around Marl's. If I were writing this very real life into a story, how would I write it? Maybe an ambulance would pass by, or the light would have character a certain way. I'd relate my struggles to the worker or to something cosmic, or possibly just to the sea.

"I'm not the kind of person to go around knocking with my sob story," I said to her, keeping my voice down, "for anybody to hear. I feel I can reveal more by writing stories in the tradition of hard-core, maybe weird literature, rooted in something old and unknown, and infusing it with my life and where I come from, as unintentionally as possible."

"Yeah, but that's what people want to read, want to hear about: the pain of others, and how they got past that pain. That's really all people want to talk to you about, too—they want somebody to listen to the painful stories of their painful lives. I mean, you have a literary agent, right? That's what these people don't have that you've got. Somebody who could sell your story real fast if you wrote it."

"That's right. I do."

"And do they know you're skimping them out like this?"

"I don't think that's how it works. An agent doesn't really tell you what to work on."

"Hold up: Who's your agent? I need to know. 'Cause I'm gonna call them and tell them their employee here—"

"Client."

"—your *client* here is skimping you out on this money-making, tear-jerking book. And, frankly, to the rest of us—like Schroeder, me, or even the bakers and baristas working here in this bakery, scared as shit about what's going on in this world and the future—this is downright insulting.

Because none of us here can probably even spell, or use a comma or an apostrophe, without having extreme reservations. So cry your sob story on the page, and do it for the rest of us who don't have that option. Do it for my sister. Or do it for your Nostradamus baby. Your one child."

On my walk home, with the cash in my coat pocket, I reflected on how I'd gotten into this arrangement with Andi, and whether my getting involved was affecting Denorah. I dropped by her shop, Little Willows Vintage. Her shift was still going on, and when I got there I said hello to her employee Marka, then crept toward the back office. I knocked twice, walked in, and was a bit surprised to find Denorah playing darts.

As if she'd been expecting me, Denorah said, "Check this out," and winked. There was a spittoon on the ground that she spit into, and then in rapid succession launched three yellow darts at a board on the opposite wall, about ten feet away. She got two bull's-eyes, and the third clipped a piece of the metal that held the corkboard together and bounced off.

Impressed, and not knowing what else to say, I said, "You chew tobacco?"

Denorah laughed and said, "I mean, I don't really chew tobacco. We just decided to keep this wicked spittoon for the store. Isn't it cute? So, sure, every once in a while me and Marka chew it. Isn't that right, Marka?" she yelled.

"We sometimes chew it," Marka yelled from the front of the shop, "but only the good shit."

"Only the good shit. I thought you knew."

"Maybe," I said. "Maybe you told me and I just forgot. Or I wasn't paying attention. I'm always zoned out all the time."

Denorah's shift ended, and on our walk I confessed to her I'd been having weird dreams out of frustration about these gigs with Andi.

"Are they about the eighteen nineties again?" she asked, right before proposing we go to a cafeteria within our budget to talk about our inner lives away from home. "It seems like we never get these moments as a couple anymore. We are either at home or coming to and from work, the market, and it's hard to break away," she said.

After ordering our initial drinks and entrées, I told Denorah that she'd guessed correctly, and that I'd been frustrated and having bad dreams owing to the vision of the 1890s that Miss Spencer was working on for her historical romance epic. In Miss Spencer's story, a young Mexican boy falls in love with a young Anglo girl who's originally from Wyoming. Even without being an expert on Mexican culture or the Southwest, I knew the racial dynamics in her story were gravely wrong. Her protagonists meet in an unlikely ballroom, where Mexicans and Anglos mix, dance, and celebrate. Plus, everyone speaks modern English, since Miss Spencer was one of the few aspiring writers I met with who actually wrote pages, filled with blatant historical anachronisms that bordered on steampunk. She'd shrug them off and remind me that she was writing fiction—make-believe— and that at her age she didn't have time to get things completely right. All that was important to her was having a finished, printed book. Miss Spencer had changed her title from "Brown Raindrops" to "Unspooled Heart" to "Orchard of Love," and currently she'd put two of them together as "Orchard Heart," with the subtitle "An Epic Romance."

After talking about it with Denorah and watching her chuckle, I could see how in the grand scheme of things this was fine. I was getting paid a great hourly wage to listen to stories and wasn't obligated to read pages—true. But sometimes people like Miss Spencer guilted me into reading them, and it was hard to decline, I said to Denorah.

"C'mon," she said. "How hard can it be? Just kick her ass a little while telling her what she wants to hear: that her stuff is mind-blowing and she has great potential. Remember that people always reward potential over a finished product, so just keep it going. People's unwritten work has potential because it doesn't exist—you don't have to face the music of editing and publishing and dealing with a finished manuscript."

After dinner, Denorah and I agreed that she should talk to Andi about picking up some of my gigs. I warned her she might hate it, but I could see how she could actually be good at it, since Denorah had attended a graduate creative writing program herself years ago, and was sensitive about giving criticism.

Within a few weeks I went from consulting with eight aspiring writers to five, and though the income I brought in took a hit, I really didn't mind, since it gave me more time for my own reading and writing. Andi transferred my meetings with Miss Spencer to Denorah, whom I was happy to see very energetic, helping brainstorm Miss Spencer's sordid vision of the late nineteenth century. Having someone to talk to about this strange way of making money changed things up for me. Denorah and I had plenty of awkward but ultimately fulfilling conversations about ageism, and why it was mostly retired, well-off people who wanted their stories told.

One afternoon, while having lunch with us, Andi told us she'd been attending literary cocktail parties, networking with people, and that she'd recruited other authors to help aspiring writers with their projects. When Denorah asked if she'd recruited anyone we knew, Andi mentioned the name of a popular author who lived in town, and whom I'd run into on occasion. He'd written a realist novel about scholars in love over the span of three decades, and it had been shortlisted for all the major awards a few years back.

For the remainder of that evening, I wasn't able to concentrate or think about anything else. Him? Andi had recruited *him*? A writer who'd brought in a huge advance, extra money from speaking engagements, awards, and possible future book contracts? If he was hard up here in the city, I thought, what were the chances for a writer who wrote weird stories, like me?

Inwardly, from that moment on, I was rattled.

I was walking out of Yeyo's Donuts after meeting with my favorite aspiring writer, Lenore Weaver, whose project was a futuristic love story set in a totalitarian tourist trap by a beach. She'd confessed to me that the story was a way of writing about a time before her marriage and, of course, way before her husband's death, when she'd met a nice brown man and fallen in love with him, which—she emphasized—had been even more controversial in those days. Lenore was my favorite because, although her project was obviously problematic, I could see she was only trying to psychologically make peace with this important experience in a way that wouldn't shock her children and friends if they were to read the work. Because she didn't particularly care about the sci-fi or speculative elements, she'd created this absurd, complex setting by a beach, and outlined scenes that cracked me up all the time. The beach town had an economy based on crystals, and unnamed streets with monuments in different corners, so that if someone gave directions, they'd explain which monument on the street was closest.

This made Lenore the most visionary and original of my clients, and though there were a lot of racist tropes within her work, I stuck to meeting with her because I knew the manuscript wouldn't stand a chance at publication. Denorah said that, to the contrary, these things were exactly the reasons somebody would publish it, and though I knew she said this jokingly, I feared more and more that she was right. Denorah also pointed out the similarities between Miss Spencer's and Lenore's narratives: they both involved an interracial relationship between a brown man and a white woman.

At any rate, I was leaving Yeyo's Donuts, and there he

was, the popular and successful author Andi had recruited, walking down the sidewalk.

He was short—just as short as I'd remembered him being. But perhaps that's unfair, because I'm a tall person. I walked about fifteen paces behind him and watched as he listened to something through his AirPods, not looking into shops, perhaps making his way to an appointment with one of Andi's writers. I stopped to read the headlines in the newspaper dispensers, to make sure the writer and I wouldn't get stuck waiting together at the crosswalk, and when the light turned, he crossed. As much as I wanted to read more than what the urgent headlines had to offer, I hurried so as not to hit a red light and fall behind.

When I thought I'd lost sight of him, I spotted his vague outline getting in line at the coffee shop on the corner. For a moment I considered going in, then realized I'd have to exchange formalities with him if he saw me.

As I walked away, I felt a creative emptiness that took me back to the early days, when I was young and dreaming of having a body of work but hadn't yet written a single page I was happy with. Things felt futile now, and glancing once more at the newspaper headlines, I could see how nothing could outdo these real-life absurdities; but perhaps living in a society where realism is the reigning literary form renders that society powerless against its own absurdity. Strange stories had helped me give meaning to the painful moments of survival, and strange stories were the only things I could continue feeding into the machine.

Moments later, when I saw Julia, my friend from Santiago, she couldn't believe the headlines either, and she stopped me, happy to run into a fellow writer who more or less understood her Spanish, and said, "Amigo, we should all be getting gas masks. Let's burn them. Burn them all down. Remember, the state is already mobilizing. They'll have tear gas and shields, but the gas masks make us unstoppable. What is everyone doing—are we just going to take this? Where's the town square around here, where do people go to mobilize? The capital? That's where I'm going. If my friends from back home were all here, forget it, tío . . ."

From down the hallway I could smell the garbanzo stew we'd made the previous evening, and could hear Andi's voice as if it were coming through the air vents. The apartment door was cracked open and I walked in to Andi laughing loudly from the kitchen and Denorah stirring the pot. The three of us sat and had the last of the stew after I cut some parsley and cilantro for garnishes.

Andi had enrolled in community college and was in a good mood because some of her credits from years back had transferred over. She'd decided to study economics, and was telling us the little things she'd learned from this aspiring-writers racket. Andi pontificated and sometimes said crass things about the cruelties of having creative aspirations, without considering that she might hurt Denorah's and my feelings.

When I directed a comment to Andi, she brushed off my words, something she'd never done before, and I saw that

Denorah noticed this, too, when Andi interrupted her a couple of times. Denorah picked at her right eyelashes—a clear sign to me that she felt uncomfortable. Finally, Andi said, "It's awkward, yes, it's awkward that most of these folks who want their stories told are older. They have the money and their kids are all grown up. The 'greatest generation.' They had careers and married during one of the greatest economic booms in history. And meanwhile, look at us here. Where even the most celebrated young writers rely on either the, um . . . empathy or altruism of the older generation. Or, in this case, their vanity. So the young writers can make enough money just to survive, we have to convince this generation that whatever sacrifices they made were worth it, and now that they have the time, they can tell their story—we can help them tell it."

"That's a slippery take, though, Andi," said Denorah.

Hearing this, Andi smiled, sipped the rest of her broth.

"What's the matter with you?" Denorah said. "You've been acting strange since you got here. Are you okay?"

Denorah made Andi tear up with these words, as if they had triggered something that went back deep into their childhood.

"You guys," Andi said, in a lower voice, "I honestly haven't been able to hear well the past few days. I can't go to the doctor and I can't see the campus nurse 'cause I'm not full-time yet. I'm scared."

Denorah shot me a look and immediately I knew: it was getting to be that season again. She stood up from her kitchen chair and said, "Hey, Andi," pretty loudly. "Andi! Tilt your head like this and with your fingers press here, between your jawbone and your ear. Do you feel anything?"

Andi tried and shook her head, disappointed. "I mean, what? Oh, you know. I feel—I think I feel something squishing, oh my god, like there's a little muddy foot in there."

I grabbed the bottle of hydrogen peroxide from the medicine cabinet, let it sit in a bowl of warm water, and, ceremoniously, Denorah brought out the little box with our Nostradamus baby. Denorah, Andi, and I took turns pouring hydrogen peroxide into our ears as we lay on our sides, and had the utmost patience with one another. I felt the crackle and fizz in my ears, and Andi kept giggling as if tiny fingers were tickling the inside of her skull.

Using paper towels, we cleaned the hydrogen peroxide residue from around our ears, necks, and hair. While watching a documentary on the history of potato chips, we waited. I offered Andi a drink, then remembered she'd been clean for a better chunk of the past year; as Denorah shut off the doc, we migrated to the chairs in the living room.

On the table facing us was our beloved creation: our Nostradamus baby. Using a tiny flashlight, Denorah took a look in Andi's right ear. Andi had her head tilted and looked very lovely, with a frightened expression.

Then Denorah said, "Oh my god, oh my god—"

"What, what," Andi said, trying not to lose her balance on the old wooden chair.

"Andi, just reach into your ear real careful. You have a lot going on in there."

Slowly, with her half-bitten nails, she pinched into her

ear, and seconds later pulled out what looked like a ball of coagulated honey with a tail: the buildup of wax that had been clogging her hearing. The three of us were impressed, and I congratulated Andi. Denorah was the one who produced the least wax, but that made sense, because her hearing had been excellent recently. What I produced was relatively minor, too, and Denorah suggested it wasn't the right time for us. Both of Andi's ears, however, ejected the same impressive amount of wax. It was wonderful to watch those two balls of wax become one, as Andi rolled them together using a circular motion with the palms of her hands.

Before we had biscuits and coffee, we agreed to perform the ceremony all the way through, and I was the first to add my wax to our baby. I did so on the little feet, which it looked like the past year had been cruel to; Denorah added hers to the liver area.

When it was Andi's turn, she said to us, "So I can just add it wherever?"

Even after we said yes, there was still hesitation in Andi. For a few seconds, watching as she decided, I thought a deep love would emerge from Andi, and she would run off with our baby. I asked myself what I would do; if I was the type of person to chase my sister-in-law down the street for my child.

Andi had her back to me and I didn't catch her adding the wax to our Nostradamus baby. When she stepped back and all of us gathered around it in a circle, our little miracle looked full-bodied, growing, and better than ever, with Andi's offering giving it a more pronounced head. For the first time, I felt what it must be like to be a proud father. I knew the world was falling apart everywhere. But in this moment—sitting with my family in the living room—I felt that a bright future was possible. The struggles of today were all worth it.

"I see now," Andi said. "I can see all this very clear now. And I can honestly say that I am a proud tía."

Denorah and I held hands. Obviously, this meant a lot to us.

The water finished boiling and I had to remind everyone that we had no sugar or milk.

"That's cool," Andi said. "The less sugar and milk, the better."

POSSUMS

Whenever I visit back home and run into possums,
I sometimes can't help myself and regress to a
most primitive state. I start throwing rocks at the
possums, stamping down one foot to scare them away. Make
loud sounds very unlike actual words to add to the theater.
Possums and I, like all the other folks back home, have a
difficult history. One time, straight out of high school, possums convinced us to enroll in a vocational class and learn
to make air-conditioning ducts and shafts. A lot of air-
conditioned buildings were popping up all over, they said.
Somebody's gotta be making the ducts and shafts. Another
time we skipped a whole month's worth of class to get stoned
and drive around listening to the same records over and over.
We'd kill a sixer driving up and down Jim Hogg County,
singing out loud, smoking joints. It's strange to romanticize
those difficult days, but here we are. I have to remind myself
that possums were the ones spreading the rumor that this

land wasn't this land anymore, that this land was now *that* land. Even though you could be standing on this land, you'd have to say, *I'm standing on* that *land*, which belonged now to those over there. It took a few years for this to be straightened out, and by then everyone had forgotten who'd started the confusion, anyway. But a few of us remembered, and we had to remind one another and ourselves every day that it was the possums who had started all this.

The possums lay low for a few years afterward—around the time kids started playing this rolling-dice game and betting flowers in the streets. Soon possums started writing and publishing tell-all books about one another, and people openly said, "Serves them right." Everyone read them, since each book was more cutting and revealing than the last. People lined up around the block on release days. Bookstores hadn't seen anything like it. A real phenomenon, everyone agreed. So now all is good with possums and the way of life back home.

Last time I was down there for a visit, I wandered off in the middle of the night and ended up at Perlitas Bar, where, at a table by the jukebox blaring José José, a possum sat, having a drink. I noticed a notebook in which the possum was writing furiously. I asked if I could sit across the same table and the possum nodded. For a while I just sat there reading my book, then after my second drink we got to talking—I stared into those eyes, like tiny stones dipped in ink, and as the night progressed the ink dripped out, and those eyes widened like a fault line in the ocean ripping open. From the fault emerged two hazy figures, like smoke out of an air shaft. The figures requested that I follow them in, and inside the possum's eyes the dark, smoky figures and I had herbal tea. In the most polite manner, they suggested I tell nobody what I knew about possums. That it was in nobody's best interest to know. And, besides, everyone would find out soon enough—for there was a tell-all book about to be published that would recount everything that had transpired. When I asked the hazy figures to elaborate, they insisted they couldn't, for they were both under contract with the publishing company, and weren't at liberty to disclose anything else.

The following day I left the border, and since the possums ran their campaign and got elected, I have not returned.

A PORTRAIT OF SIMÓN BOLÍVAR BUCKNER

Gabriel got a call from Swedish Hill, Texas, to drive to an abandoned luxury resort once named Lunar Winds. Before the First World War, it'd been a popular getaway for rich people with pulmonary diseases, then went bankrupt after the advent of penicillin and other antibiotics. The woman who'd phoned couldn't meet him, but she nailed instructions to the door, directing him through the resort to the outdoor stage.

Workers had started knocking down the stage piece by piece, she'd explained, only to discover a hive of bees about eight feet tall and fifteen feet wide behind a wall. When he reached the spot, Gabriel folded the instructions away, whistled, and clapped once at the sight of the hive. He held up his camera and snapped several photographs. He saw signs of roaches and rat feces only on stage right—the rest of the hive looked thick with bees and good honey.

Gabriel walked back to his truck through the cobwebbed

hallway—the insides of the building looked more like a piece of land trying to keep living after a terrible brush fire; all the shattered glass from the windows had turned to sand long ago. He grew excited at the sight of a big hive like that, and the usual thoughts went through his mind: the life all the bees were creating, everything lost in the land they were trying, again and again, to weave together. He felt that the honey the bees had accumulated represented something deeper, something he associated with the neighborhood or family that lived near where the hive had been found—in this case, the people who had stayed at this once-famous resort.

Facing the stage in his beekeeping suit, Gabriel walked with his gear toward the hive. This is what our brains are like, thought Gabriel: giant hives even bigger than this, and each one of these bees is a little something about us, a little memory, tic, or desire—some are bad, but most are good.

He wanted to salvage the good honey, and, using a pick, he stabbed out slabs into thick plastic bags, filled two of them, then started arduously removing the hive. It was a full day's work, and he found the bees to be as aggressive as he'd expected.

Gabriel managed to break off large chunks of the hive intact, then shelved them in the back of his truck one by one, the bees clinging to their home and defending it the whole way. He took a long look at the outdoor stage before leaving, and noticed that perhaps it was more accommodating to theater than to musical performances. Walking through the main vestibule of the resort, admiring the Gothic columns holding up the roof, he noticed an old painting hanging over the fireplace—through the grime of time Gabriel made out the portrait of a gray old man with wild facial hair, wearing some kind of military uniform. Possibly from the Civil War, though he didn't recognize him as one of that war's generals.

Gabriel drove back to his little headquarters in town, an hour and a half away, and listened to the classical music station, which he rarely did. Somewhere he saw a sign that read FOREST FOR SALE, and for a couple of miles this confused him.

He relocated the hive for a few extra dollars at the apiary by the Dollar General, and on the drive back to his apartment he called his mother on his flip phone. He considered telling her about the hive, but when he had the chance, Gabriel refrained.

At his apartment he messily transferred the coagulated honey from the two bags into three seventy-two-ounce glass containers, sealed them, showered, then went to bed.

Gabriel was physically and emotionally worn out.

That night he had a dream he wouldn't remember upon awaking. The dream ended with a glassy blue wall in a mansion, but before that it was a planet, and before that the seven seas; before that it was one ocean, a lake, then a lagoon; before that it was a pond, then a puddle, and finally a drop that dripped in an art gallery over the open casket of a man wearing an epaulet, clutching a dictionary or maybe a cutlass blade. Before that he had been wheeled in, passed out on a wheelbarrow, before tasting the eternal soup, the stones having turned to meat, and the wolf dug up a radish. Before that, the man wore huaraches and with a snore harangued nothing less than what needed to be harangued; his voice charged as if riding a horse running backward, the horse was a shadow, and the boom clapped loudly from the man's nostril-like eyes. A silver light emanated from his face as if it were plated in nickel, before turning to copper dust, screaming, "Copper is the royal element in dreams!" Before that it was a shoe, then a wagon, and it all started up as weather once again, in a way that seemed to drain into the pasture, which turned to marble chiseled into a throne, atop a chariot, atop a light that was now orange, now fire, but before that a gelatinous fire, one that enclosed Gabriel's dream in a bubble from the very beginning in a way he was destined to forget.

The following morning, having breakfast at his favorite taco joint, Gabriel felt, in some way, spiritually unsound. He felt vaguely that his life was lacking something. It wasn't that he was single, or that his mother seemed to have aged decades in the past few years. It was something less tangible, less from the world of the senses, something that had deep psychic roots within him.

Gabriel checked his messages and found no missed calls. He finished his tacos and threw away the brown bag, walked to his truck. As he drove he told himself, I am Gabriel Spencer, the son of Eugene Spencer and Magdalene Carlisle. I am here in this world because. I am here in this world *because* . . . He accentuated the word "because," asserting it, as if the word itself could unravel his hidden destiny.

He found himself driving toward his mother's place. The truth was, a young woman had moved into an apartment close to his mother's. She had brown skin and messy dark hair. The young woman was from Bolivia and was a graduate student at the local university. Gabriel knew this because his mother had befriended her, and had even let this young woman snap photographs of her for a forthcoming art show. Though he was suspicious at first, after he exchanged a few passing smiles and hellos with her, he felt it could do no harm to have his mother make young friends and be creative at her age.

A few times he'd said her name aloud: Araseli. It had a distant ring to it, like the bounce of a gold coin, if the coin were the sun. Gabriel couldn't remember having a foreign acquaintance since he was a boy. He'd been a combination of nervous, skeptical, and shy when he first approached her; on this occasion he'd filled two fancy thirty-six-ounce jars with honey, sealed with blue lids: one for his mother, the other to start a conversation with Araseli.

Gabriel sat at a kitchen table in his mother's apartment, and mostly he listened to her as she told him, once again, about the time when she was a girl and her neighbor won every shoe at the shoe raffle in Davenport. He'd left the second jar of honey in his truck, and before leaving Gabriel set it by the door of Araseli's apartment without a note.

He didn't see Araseli until a few months later. Gabriel was carrying some of his mother's belongings from her apartment when he ran into her. She was on her way to the university, and Gabriel was holding his mother's seashell desk lamp and a suitcase of her clothes that he was planning on donating to Goodwill.

Gabriel stopped moving as Araseli walked up to him.

"Excuse me. Hello. You're Magdalene's son? I'm very sorry about your mother; I only recently found out. We knew each other only a little bit, but she always talked about you. I'm a photographer, and Magdalene was kind enough to share her story and sit for me a couple times. If there is anything I can help with, please don't hesitate to knock on my door."

Gabriel thanked her, and said he had a few more weeks on the lease of the apartment. He also casually mentioned that his mother's funeral had been small but nice, and that she was buried next to his father. Araseli lamented not knowing what had happened until it was too late, then apologized, but really had to make it to a class she was teaching.

Satisfied with his work for the day, Gabriel decided to call it quits, bought two tallboys, and headed to his apartment. After finishing the first one, he unplugged his television and set it on the curb, unplugged his personal desktop computer and did the same.

Among the things he'd carried out of and kept from his mother's place was a hardcover book no longer than a hundred pages. Lightly buzzed, and satisfied with this new absence of screens, Gabriel started reading it. He learned it was a nineteenth-century German novella, and though the translation was old, it was very simple to follow. In the novella, the main character was the composer Mozart. This confused Gabriel at first, as he didn't know if the book was based on a real period in time or if it was made-up, and he started questioning the definition of the word "fiction," after looking it up in his mother's old *American Heritage Dictionary*.

Eight pages into the story, he let go of all these doubts and surrendered unconditionally to the narrative. He sat at the small wooden table in his living room after picking up another two tallboys, and was determined to stay up finishing the book.

Shortly after nine the following morning, Gabriel awoke to a crowd of people clapping, then realized there was a storm rolling through. His hangover wasn't too bad, and after showering he opened the front door. It was really coming down. There was something holy about the squawking deluge that made Gabriel think of nothing at all. He filled a tall glass with water and sat protected by the awning, chugging, as fists of rain banged down on the world. Then Gabriel remembered the novella, grabbed it from the table, and flipped through the pages. He couldn't believe the story had moved him to tears the night before. He laughed about it, then gave it some serious thought.

Gabriel's apartment building sat on a hill, so he and his truck were safe from rising waters; he knew there'd be no work calls in this weather and decided to stay home for the day. He saw the computer and television set on the curb really getting thrashed by the rain, like a couple of statues or determined vagrants. Then, for some reason, he thought of the windows in his mother's apartment. More specifically, the windows in her bedroom. Though he knew it was absurd, Gabriel started to worry about the windows, and about water getting in, creating a draft that could make his mother sick.

He looked at his hands and they were shaking as the rain placated. Gabriel put on a shirt and his boots, and it wasn't until he turned on Datepalm that he could see how bad the rain had been while he slept. There was a Honda low on the road with water covering three-quarters of it. On its roof sat a stoic, skinny dog, and Gabriel stopped, made direct eye contact with it, before deciding the dog was close enough to the elevated curb to jump. The truck was half a block out when he changed his mind about the dog, but when he got back the Honda was still underwater and the dog was gone.

On the radio came a song called "Ain't No Grave Gonna Hold This Body Down," and though Gabriel didn't know the lyrics, he felt as if he did and turned it up as loud as he could stand. When he pulled into his mother's apartment complex, Gabriel panicked, thinking he'd forgotten the keys, but they were right there where they had always been, on his key ring. The rain started up again, and he ran toward the awning over his mother's place and opened the door. Gabriel had cleared out her belongings himself, but despite this it was a shock to see everything—all the photographs, furni-

ture, little touches that made this place his mother's—
stripped down and gone.

Gabriel felt dizzy. He'd been wondering recently about
panic attacks—what they were and what they actually felt
like—because he had been experiencing sensations he had
no other way of explaining. After walking into his mother's
bedroom and finding the windows not only closed but
latched, he stood in the middle of the empty living room,
listening to the thunderstorm, wondering if what he was
feeling—the hyperventilating, sweating, unstoppable tears,
shaking—could be described as a panic attack.

It seemed foolish, and he laughed with tears in his eyes,
but all he wanted was a person to assure him that his mother
had died—and, as he had no other close relatives, there was
nobody to tell him that what he was going through was probably normal.

The open door slowly creaked as the wind pushed it
open the rest of the way. In the doorway appeared Araseli,
holding a security guard's flashlight. She pointed the light at
the crouching man in the living room, then turned it off
when she recognized Gabriel.

"I thought you were a squatter."

"No, it's me. Don't call the police."

"Well, I wasn't going to call police on a squatter. I wanted
to see if they were okay. Maybe give them some juice, and
tell them about that house in the woods with running water,
where squatters can stay."

Gabriel was looking down the entire time, and it registered
with Araseli that he had been crying. She felt awful—didn't

know what to say. Rather than thinking of anything, or reaching to touch him in some kind of solidarity, Araseli walked back out and shut the door.

After the rain stopped, Gabriel felt worn down. He washed himself in the empty bathroom, made sure there was nothing on his teeth, and when he walked outside he found a note taped to the door that read: "Forgot to mention I'm in 216. Please come by anytime for some tea."

On his drive home, Gabriel thought about the note. If it had been written by anybody else—one of his old friends, for instance—he would've thought that inviting somebody for tea was a fancy joke. But it was definitely serious in tone, and Gabriel found it difficult to accept the invitation.

Over the following weeks he returned the apartment keys to the landlord, signed paperwork ending the lease prematurely under the death clause, and on the first Friday of the new month, he picked up the paper with the entertainment and culture sections.

He looked for ongoing art exhibitions, and was curious to find it was the closing week of A *Portrait of Simón Bolívar Buckner: Photographs by Araseli Choque* at the university art gallery.

Gabriel parked in the visitors' section, and walking the halls of the university, trying to find the gallery, he felt out of place in more than a couple of ways. It was late in the day and few students were present. Gabriel spotted a janitor blocking off a restroom and he felt relieved, as if he and the janitor were old pals. Thanks to the janitor's generous, concise directions, Gabriel found the exhibition in the building across from the covered roof, and he walked in just a half hour before the work-study student had to close it down.

In the gallery he was greeted immediately by a wall-sized black-and-white portrait of a man sitting on a couch, wearing a baseball glove, with an air-conditioner unit to his right and a pit bull to his left. A cardboard poster on an easel read the complete title: A PORTRAIT OF SIMÓN BOLÍVAR BUCKNER: PHOTOGRAPHS OF WORKING BOLIVIAN IMMIGRANTS IN THE UNITED STATES. From the artist's statement Gabriel learned these were collaborative portraits Araseli Choque had snapped and printed of different Bolivian American people she'd encountered in the United States, and she abstractly connected Bolivians to a vital part of this country as far back as the nineteenth century, when two parents in Kentucky had named their son—a future governor—Simón Bolívar.

Araseli had captured people in their homes next to objects they felt connected them to the working world in this country, and by the prints were brief statements made by the people. Gabriel read the card with the statement from the man on the couch, and it read: "I came to this country thirty six years [ago] when playing minor league baseball, then when the team ended nobody would hire me. Luckily I learned to fix air conditions and bought a trailer and my

Oldsmobile. I've found it hard to have long relationships. I haven't been to a funeral back home in over ten years."

Gabriel was impressed by the sheer size of the photographs and was a little dismayed not to find an explanation for that artistic choice in Araseli's statement. The entire show comprised twelve four-by-six-foot photographs. He looked around and soaked each one in individually. He was particularly drawn to one taken inside of what looked like an old van. It was of a couple with two children, engaged in a tranquil yet chaotic domestic situation within the van's confines. He was eager to see the caption, which read: "My parents both came here separately and worked for the transit center for many years before they met. I was the first of our family to graduate high school, then college. My husband is white. We worked in software and retired early. We teach our children to respect all cultures and the environment while camping in this country's public lands."

He walked toward the back, to a photograph of a dark, middle-aged man in shorts and a T-shirt, next to a light-skinned man wearing a suit, both sitting on chairs by the sea. The caption read: "I was born in the South, where my parents moved together, but I left as fast as I could. Only I left to the Midwest, which is worse. Ended up here on a sales gig, where Charles and I met. He and I attended the same Spanish-speaking meet-up at the community center. My parents do okay retired. They love Charles, and Charles's parents love me."

Before looking at the neighboring portrait, Gabriel read

its caption: "My mother's parents came here a long time ago and my mother was raised to feel shame about speaking Spanish and for where she came from. I was a military bride and took from the same kind of people my parents were. I am a widow now. My son works in bees and he's my pride & joy. We've never spoken of our shared heritage."

Gabriel looked at the image under the track lights of his mother in her apartment. The lighting and depth of field made her skin look darker than he remembered it had been in the days before she unexpectedly died. By her side, on a little table, was the seashell lamp, a portrait of his father in uniform, and a big jar of honey—Gabriel recognized the jar as the one he'd left for Araseli without an explanation months ago.

He couldn't remember later how he had managed it, but Gabriel, carefully, without losing his balance, walked out of the gallery, and with an effortlessness he took for granted, found the visitors' parking lot and his truck, and drove away from the university. He remembered he had to eat and somehow ordered a burger with no fries at the drive-through, took it home, and left it on the table.

The next morning he microwaved the burger and everything felt fine.

The humidity arrived and Gabriel received more than the usual number of calls about hives. He safely removed a hive covered in roaches from the bell tower of the old church.

One from the Gas Works plant, which the workers had been spraying with various oils and fluids, so the bees were either livid or dead. One from the old copy room at McAllister Elementary, which explained the buzzing the students and faculty had reported hearing, and when he took a look around the property he found a few more.

At odd times of the day, Gabriel found himself reflecting on his vocation. His mother had encouraged him to apprentice with Old Man Hogan, after his health problems left him unable to do it all himself. Like Gabriel was now, Hogan had been the on-call bee wrangler in all five surrounding counties, and had professional ties to beekeepers who gave him jobs delivering honey when the bees were gone for the season. After high school and his father's illness, Gabriel had stuck with the job while living at home, since he hadn't wanted to continue with school. When his father passed away and they'd had to sell the house, Gabriel lived alone, away from his parents in an apartment, for the first time.

Distanced from it all, Gabriel remembered a little detail from the exhibit at the university gallery, of the couple who had met at a meet-up for Spanish speakers. Gabriel wondered if there could be something similar for people interested in sign language, which was something he'd always wanted to learn more of and discuss.

He also considered joining an internet dating service, and using a computer at the library, Gabriel started a profile with an uploaded photo that was honest about his receding hairline. But he logged in only a couple of times; he was too embarrassed to reach out to anybody, and was ashamed nobody was reaching out to him.

After putting it off as long as he could, Gabriel was forced to upgrade his phone because of the phone company's technology upgrade, and on a call to Swedish Hill, Texas, he tried the GPS feature. When he arrived at the Alamo Springs, there was the manager to meet him by the door. Gabriel admired the complete renovation they'd done on the old Lunar Winds since he'd last been there. He'd read about it in the paper but hadn't been aware that it was already up and running.

New cars were parked up and down the modest parking lot, and Gabriel wondered which ones belonged to the employees. The moss and mildew had been scraped clean, the building repainted; tall magnolias and cedars only made its fifteen stories seem larger. The manager went through his familiar routine about the improvements and features of the building as they walked down a long hallway.

Gabriel had left his suit and gear in the truck. Eventually, the manager got right down to it, and broke into stories of escalating encounters with the bees. They had made it to the main vestibule the long way, as the main door was being repaired. Through the many windows Gabriel could see a group of people doing various calm activities in an impressive flowering garden near where he'd removed the original hive, but there was no sign of the old stage. The people ranged in age from teenagers to adults, and Gabriel was convinced they had one thing in common: they were all younger than him.

"Are those people family? Of the people staying here?"

"No," said the manager. "Those are some of our patients."

As he looked around he noticed that the people out there wore robes and similar black shoes. Thinking back on all the hospitals and treatment centers he and his mother had accompanied his father to, Gabriel asked, "Is this place more of a hospital than a hotel?"

The manager said, "We are a licensed facility offering alternative remedies for people who choose to abstain from vaccinations, because of the risk."

They continued walking and entered a cordoned-off area near the back, where the manager pointed to a large hearth with a tall chimney with three velvet couches and reading chairs around it, below tall bookshelves and a skylight.

"This is where all the incidents have occurred. We think they're up there in the chimney. With the winter approaching, we want to be able to use it."

Gabriel walked toward the chimney, his eyes ignoring everything but the painting hanging about ten feet over the hearth. He vaguely remembered it from the time he'd been called in to remove the large hive from the outdoor stage, and he wasn't sure if it could possibly be the same one. That seemed like lifetimes ago now, before his mother passed away. It was a mounted oil painting on canvas, not a photograph, of a man in military uniform—maybe a general, but his ranking wasn't specified. He had dark snowman's eyes and a gray beard like a dagger, about a foot long.

He asked the manager and one of the bellhops to step back about ten feet while he checked under the chimney. Gabriel saw nothing under there, to the astonishment of the manager. He eyed the bookshelves—especially the section near the portrait, where he spotted a bee on the spine of an unidentified red hardback. Gabriel excused himself, went to his truck, came back with a twelve-foot retractable ladder, and climbed it.

He removed a couple of books from the shelf, but saw nothing.

Gabriel climbed back down and stood next to the manager and the bellhop, who were both puzzled and now personally invested in this mystery.

Feeling he was making eye contact with the portrait, Gabriel said, "Is there a particular time of day when the bee encounters happen? Or does something specific usually go on?"

The manager and the bellhop looked at each other and said there was nothing they could think of.

From the desk across the vestibule a *ding* was heard, signaling the bellhop for his services; a fistful of bees emerged from the back of the portrait over the chimney, and hovered around.

"This guy," said Gabriel, smiling.

Wearing only his blue jeans and T-shirt, without his suit, he climbed the ladder. When he came face-to-face with the portrait, the bees were buzzing and circling, as if they were the general's aura, or his guardians.

"Who are you?" Gabriel said quietly into the portrait's

eyes. He peeked behind the painting. The frame was old and well crafted—there was a deep space in the back and the bees had made a very good home of it. Gabriel knew the bees were getting to be slower at this time of year, so he merely grabbed the portrait, despite the reservations expressed by the manager, and unhinged it.

He'd always been good at keeping his balance despite awkward angles, and stepped down the ladder with the portrait, the bees flying everywhere, like tiny warplanes attempting to shoot Gabriel down. One stung him on the arm, then one stung his neck. "So sorry, dears," he whispered to them. Gabriel swung the portrait toward the manager, asked him, "Do you know who this is in the painting here?"

The manager stepped farther back and shook his head—the bees looked angry. "I know someone who does. I can ask."

Gabriel held the painting up as if he wanted to show it off, but he was admiring the clean hive the bees had built behind it—he wondered how they were getting out of the building, then thought of the hive as looking into the mind of the general; the bees were every one of his brain cells, keeping him alive. As the bellhop walked back from his task, he saw the portrait in Gabriel's hands and the buzzing bees going wild. Gabriel swung it around and asked, "Do you know who this is a portrait of?"

Defending the hive to their deaths, the bees buried their stingers in Gabriel, one in his forehead, another in his cheek, one in his upper lip, and like ten in each arm. To the bellhop it looked like the bees were coming simultaneously from the beard of the portrait and the face of this bee wrangler they'd called in.

The bellhop, sweating, shook his head.

Gabriel turned to the people seeking alternative remedies out in the garden and, to the protestations of the manager, walked toward them, determined to find out the name of the painting's sitter.

ROPA USADA

assie knew she could make extra money selling vintage clothing on the internet, so in her first semester out of grad school, she drove to Chulas Fronteras Ropa Usada, down by the border in the *maquiladora* district.

The bouncer at the door weighed Cassie on a scale as a shoplifting precaution, and handed her a ticket, along with a map of the enormous warehouse. She was originally from the border and so she said "no, thanks" to the map, since she knew her way around well, and walked inside. There were hills of denim, with polyester, wool, and old jeans compacted, forming different roads. Fans as tall as Cassie were blowing everywhere like electric windmills, creating metallic cyclones that howled over the exclamations of people—mostly brown women like herself, but many with young children—picking through the used clothing.

Cassie began sweating, and from the clothes on the ground she felt steam rising, as if the ghosts trapped in the clothes were sweating, too. She took a purple envelope out of her dress pocket, just to make sure she hadn't forgotten it, to make sure it was really there.

Cassie followed the denim road, expecting a silk scarecrow or barkcloth lion to jump out at any moment—then she remembered that the outside rules didn't apply at the ropa usada. She saw about ten women on the crest of a hill of used clothes, pulling sleeves and khaki legs from under their feet like ripe carrots. Three kids were huddled down on the ground by a fan, with their six eyes immersed in a book, the child in the middle holding it open. Cassie saw the book consisted of complicated epic verse, and she kept walking and spotted the train to take her to the other end, but discovered it wasn't running.

So Cassie walked through the hills of clothes that rose and fell, until she reached a corner of the ropa usada she'd never visited. Cassie regretted not taking a map from the bouncer. She came across a man looking at an unfolded map under the threshold of a little den made of sports-team jackets; they were jackets of teams that no longer existed, like the Washington Bullets, the Houston Oilers, and the Oakland Raiders.

Cassie said to the man, "Can I please borrow your map real quick when you're done looking at it, sir? I'm afraid I don't know where I am."

"Don't you come near me," he said, and hid behind a curtain of hockey and Little League jerseys.

Cassie heard a racket—the terrain suddenly changed from

denim to corduroy. It got darker in the ropa usada and the fans became scarcer. Cassie was really sweating now; she felt queasy, and took a break to hydrate and eat lunch. She unpacked her veggie tacos, sat on a mound of hoodies, and had her meal as the racket seemed to be getting closer and closer. A crowd of people moved both laterally and in a circle, like a tornado, very near her, and she wrapped her food up.

Cassie approached two young women and yelled over everyone, "What's happening?"

The young woman wearing hoop earrings and with a lip piercing yelled back, "They found a rare Tropinini blazer! Somebody just bid on it for a lot on the internet!"

As she processed this information, the tornado of people moved away toward the satin moors and a distant exit. Cassie kept walking, and followed the northern bulb in the otherwise-dark, depthless ceiling. Though she never seemed to get closer to the light, Cassie felt she was nearing her destination upon hearing the unmistakable sound of castanets. Cassie knew this meant the City Girls were nearby—they'd probably already surrounded her, hidden in the brush of gloves, because when she looked around, Cassie realized she was in the part of the ropa usada with nothing but gloves. For small hands and big hands, puffy gloves and long gloves, bright gloves, mittens, and amputated gloves. The gloves became vegetation and their own ecosystem. Branches of gloves hung from glove-trees, and they longed to touch Cassie's face and body, but she slapped them away as she pushed through their thick woods.

The castanets became louder. Cassie reached a clearing of handkerchiefs and a voice said, "Well, if it isn't our old friend Cassandra."

It was the voice of the City Girls, who ruled the internet vintage clothing market, thanks not only to this particular ropa usada, but to all of them throughout the South. If you wanted to sell clothes on the internet without any trouble, there was a tribute to be paid to the City Girls. Cassie had had a troublesome relationship with them in the past, and after she got into grad school she swore she'd never deal with them again. It'd been a while since Cassie had seen them. As they circled her, she remembered the most obvious thing about them, which was that the City Girls looked like supermodels. Though their style was one Cassie felt was very conventional and capitalist, she couldn't help wanting to weep at their collective blinding beauty, and fought to hold it together and stand her ground before them.

"Did you bring what belongs to us," the City Girls asked, in that mechanical way they spoke, in unison, like a Greek chorus.

Cassie pulled out the purple envelope she'd brought and said, "Count it. It's all there."

The City Girls were pleased at this and said, "No need. We trust you. Yet we also know you inwardly judge us. Because unlike other people who are just buying clothes here for their families, we are here to find the good stuff people throw away. We can tell the good hand-stitching from the bad machine stuff. All the big cities thrive on the clothes we find here. And even though you aspire to be like us, you inwardly judge us. For shame. For shame," they whispered, then screamed, not in unison, but one by one.

Parting from one another, the City Girls wheeled through a lounge cart with a deep bowl and a silver platter. "You know what happens now," the City Girls said to Cassie, who knew this was coming. "You powder our doughnut."

The platter was uncovered to reveal a small brown doughnut sitting on a plate like an ugly duckling. The deep bowl beside it was filled with a white powder. Cassie grabbed the doughnut and did the deed while in ecstatic glee the City Girls hissed, "Yes. Yes. Powder our doughnut. Powder it."

When Cassie was finished and every last spot on the doughnut was covered, the City Girls split it up into even pieces and ate the powdered doughnut.

Breathing heavily, and thoroughly fulfilled, the City Girls needed a cigarette, and afterward, a nap. "Go now," the City Girls said, as they each found a different handkerchief mound to pass out on. "You can sell clothes on the internet without the shakedown."

Cassie walked away as they fell into slumber; for a moment they looked harmless, as if, once surrounded by that wreckage of used clothing, the City Girls weren't in charge of who ate and who starved in the vintage-clothes-selling racket. Cassie had lived in the city for over ten years now, and she dwelled on the reasons why she'd never be made a City Girl; then, feeling she was taking a stance, told herself she would never become a City Girl even if given the opportunity.

She lost track of time, heading in the vague direction of

an exit, and everything around was flannel. Cassie tried to remember the clothing on her wish list for her internet store. Though the powdered-doughnut incident had made her nauseated, hunger was overtaking Cassie once again. The distant chime of a bell resounded and the thick humidity of the ropa usada became only thicker. Cassie couldn't remember when the last time was that she'd even seen a fan.

The smoke was slight at first—Cassie wondered if it even was smoke, then saw the trash bin emitting white fire and white smoke, with meat unlike anything she'd ever seen roasting over it.

Small houses made of broomsticks, parkas, and cheap coats lined both ends of a short road. A woman was ringing a bell that was hanging on a brick tower. Cassie had heard of the village in the ropa usada, but, like everybody else, had always known to stay away. Since she was wandering without a map, she'd stumbled upon it by accident, and Cassie walked right up to the woman ringing the bell. The woman had bandages around her eyes, and Cassie concluded she must be blind.

The woman stopped pulling the rope that rang the bell and yelled, "Harold, your bride has arrived."

Cassie looked around and couldn't see this bride the woman was referring to.

"Excuse me," she said to the woman.

From one of the little houses, the one made of suit jackets three stories high, came a tall man with shaggy hair that covered his eyes. Cassie couldn't tell if he also had his eyes bandaged, but he seemed to have no trouble finding his way around.

"Is she the one," Harold said, moving his head up and down, checking out Cassie. "Is she the one you gave your eyes for, Mother? Is she?"

Laughter came from one of the parka houses, and across the street a couple were heard arguing while a child cried.

Cassie shook her head—wanted to scream No—and the flannel under her feet became unsteady, as if the clothes were beginning to slide in an avalanche.

The wave of clothing was fifty feet away when she saw it.

T-shirts of old bands and businesses, discarded quinceañera dresses, pearl snap shirts, denim in every form, jackets, polo shirts, school uniforms, scarves, boots, chanclas, high heels, ties, sneakers, Oxfords with worn soles in every size, long skirts, miniskirts, shawls, aprons, galoshes, tank tops, bathrobes, leather jackets, vests, belts, suspenders, ruffled blouses, tunics, hooded sweatshirts, earmuffs, all styles of hat, and every snarky saying ever printed on 60 percent polyester, 40 percent cotton came together like the earth had quaked from deep in its depths. Cassie was taken by the tsunami of clothes, as if the distant levee holding pallets and pallets of them had finally burst—she tumbled and nearly drowned many times, but managed to grab hold of a floating desk chair as the sea of clothes gurgled and shifted.

Before her eyes flashed the reasons she'd come out here in the first place: her debts and student loans, which had started being deducted automatically from her bank account every month, no matter what. As the clothes slowly came to a muddy halt, Cassie stood and dusted herself off.

I'm alive, Cassie thought.

It made her sad to think that, in what she felt were her final moments, what tumbled through her mind was all the money she owed: not her mother, her family, the people she loved, or the possessions she held dear, but her crushing debt.

Cassie saw that her slippers were gone and, barefoot, she went looking for survivors.

The *clipetty-clopetty* of a horse moved toward her and a foggy voice yelled, "Report the dead. Report the dead." Cassie watched as the horse-drawn wagon passed by, hauling a pile of dead bodies.

Wails and moans came from deep within the clothes. Cassie saw two legs sticking out of a clothing dune, clearly tussling to get their torso and head out. Cassie walked up and carefully grabbed one foot. The person fought against it, then must have sensed good intentions because they let Cassie grab the other foot, and she pulled without further struggle.

Like a thorn being pinched from a wound, Harold's body emerged from the dune of clothing.

"My bride," Harold said, walking on his knees toward Cassie.

"I can't marry you, Harold," she said. In a flight of improvisation, she added: "The truth is that I'm already taken."

Sitting on the beach of clothing like a stranded mariner, Harold started to loudly weep. "I've lost it all," he said, "and you deny me even this?"

Cassie knew better than to fall for the trap of consolation, so she said, "It's for your own good, sweetie," and went looking for the exit.

The terrain had changed. The old polyester, wool, and denim roads were all destroyed. Cassie looked down at her dark feet—though there were shoes her size everywhere, she didn't want to walk in any of them. Up ahead there was a bright light, and the train was still sitting there, broken-down, unaware of the disasters that had occurred.

The ground of clothing below her became concrete, then eventually tile.

Cassie saw her reflection on the wall-sized mirror near the entrance as she walked by. She didn't recognize the clothing she wore—somewhere inside, her wardrobe had changed, unbeknownst to her. It looked like she'd even lost weight.

The bouncer saw her walking up. Though he'd developed a thick skin in this business, Cassie's staticky hair, dirty face, and just-got-off-the-UFO stare warmed his heart. He noticed she had bought no clothes, asked for her ticket, and, as a shoplifting precaution, weighed her again.

He was holding a fur coat and said, "Someone tried shoplifting this Gianni mink coat from us a while ago. My manager's not here right now and it's cold out there. Since you're a few pounds lighter than how you came in, why don't you have it?"

Cassie tried to smile as the bouncer snuggled the coat

around her shoulders. She couldn't think of the words for "thank you," and walked outside. It was snowing. Barefoot, she walked to her car and started it. Cassie wondered how long she'd been at the ropa usada. She drove away and thought the bouncer had been nice to give her the coat. As she surfed for a radio station, Cassie said aloud, "It's people like that man who are keeping this world going, holding it together." Then, when she had found her song, she wondered what a Gianni mink coat like this could go for on the internet.

PANCHOFIRE & MARINA

ast night, after finally watching the documentary on the unsolved murder of the young nurse in South Texas, I realized all I had was a can of tuna in the pantry—in the fridge was half an onion, some mustard, and a nearly empty carton of expired milk.

Looked in all the drawers for the can opener with no luck, then, using a kitchen knife, stabbed all along the can's edge, the tin cringing like a viola popping strings. When I'd cleared nearly half the can, I pried it open with a fork and thought, How funny, remembering the days I'd lived next to Father Chabelo Andrade in the east side, while forcing clumps of tuna into my mouth.

His name was never mentioned in the documentary entitled *Preying on the Holy*. But, since I'd known Father Andrade personally, and was only now piecing together the events that occurred back in 1957, it didn't surprise me.

When I learned about the documentary, it had interested me because the murder took place in South Texas, close to where I'm from. It begins as the story of a young Mexican American woman, the studious and charismatic Linda Salazar. She is the first person in her family to receive a high school diploma, and, later, a college degree. She gets hired as a nurse at McAllen Renaissance Hospital. In her twenties, she exchanges letters with her former female classmates, which are narrated by an actress; they reveal Linda to be a romantic and pious young woman, who still wears her promise ring and goes out on dates with young doctors.

In dealing with the sick from day to day, Linda learns to love God and attends church every Sunday and Wednesday. She is described as attractive and is known in the community for dressing well. Single men attend the church, hoping to have an exchange with the young nurse. She goes to confession frequently and even befriends one of the priests, Father Sims. Linda Salazar agrees to have dinner with a young doctor after church one Ash Wednesday. That day, there is a thunderstorm before Mass. At the service, according to eyewitnesses, Linda is fidgety. Waiting in line to confess, she asks a few gentlemen if she can cut ahead, for she is in a hurry, and they modestly acquiesce.

The following day, her parents report to the authorities that she never came home, and her car is discovered at San Juditas Church. A few blocks from the church, Linda's purse is discovered in a bush with her driver's license and money intact. Six miles to the northeast, a pair of women's black dress shoes are found in the mud by the side of the road, apparently thrown from a moving vehicle, and are identified by the family as having been worn by Linda the evening she disappeared.

Five days later, her body is found by construction workers, floating along the Rio Bravo River in Anzalduas Park. The autopsy reports she has been dead for three days. Linda Salazar's blouse is ripped open and her underwear is missing; the left side of her face is bruised and swollen, as if she'd been beaten with a blunt object. Any evidence that could've identified the killer or killers has been washed away by the river. Within a week, everybody in the congregation, her family, her coworkers, and her suitors since high school are interviewed by the authorities. The name that keeps popping up is Father Sims's. She confessed to him on Ash Wednesday, and it's reported by a few people, including another priest and an acolyte, that Father Sims and Linda Salazar went off to the back room of the church for a private confession. This was not out of the ordinary, since a private confession is offered to anybody upon request.

The service ended shortly after this, and nobody saw Linda Salazar alive again except Father Sims, who, it turns out, is the youngest and least experienced priest in San Juditas. He'd come down from Tulsa, and after living for a time in Premont, made it all the way down to the Valley, in South Texas.

It is discovered that a week prior to Linda's disappearance, a male matching Father Sims's description was reported to have attacked a librarian named Estela Casas in the middle of the day, by the shrine with the votive candles in San Juditas Church. She is able to identify Father Sims as her attacker, but there's still insufficient evidence for the authorities. Father Sims denies all the allegations and has alibis that are confirmed by others for the investigators. Suspiciously, during the days after Linda's disappearance, other priests at San Juditas notice cuts and scrapes on Father Sims's hands and around his neck—they go on record saying the explanation Father Sims gave for the cuts was that he'd gotten locked out of his apartment and had a rough time climbing a tree to get through a window.

The doctor Linda had the date with is also questioned by the police, and, later, in the documentary as an old man. He is found to have a reliable alibi, and in the film he explains how this incident ruined his reputation and upward mobility for a long time. The documentary makes you believe Father Sims committed the crime and got away with it. He moves back to Tulsa the following year, continuing with the clergy— then, ten years after the death of Linda Salazar, Father Sims is found dead in a chapel, surrounded by snuffed candles and statues of the saints, his cassock stained with his own semen. He appears to have shot himself through the chest with a revolver—the weapon is found at the scene, and the incident is ruled a suicide, the events shrouding it just as mysterious and elusive to the authorities as those around Linda's death.

The documentary ends with a giant question mark: Why would this priest, Father Sims, commit suicide, and was the act related to the murder of Linda Salazar?

Why the semen?

Where did the gun come from?

Though the bulk of the evidence suggests he killed Linda, he never confesses to the crime—he moves away, doesn't change his name, lives unharassed. Then one day at the chapel he jacks off and kills himself?

It doesn't add up to the police nor to the documentarians.

What began as an ordinary mystery ends as a profound one.

Again, I was attracted to the documentary because I love a good South Texas story; ten minutes into it, I sensed something ominously familiar. Something within it emerged like a sleepy bear from the deep woods of my memory, as if the story had been reworked from an old fairy tale or myth, and I felt I had some kind of answer to it—then I remembered it wasn't me but my old neighbor from the east side—the other priest, Father Andrade—whom this story is really about.

He was an old, blind brown man who wasn't really a priest, but everybody on the block called him Father because the younger nuns of the convent Sala Sagrada had been his volunteer helpers most of his life. They maintained his house, shopped for his groceries, made sure his bills got paid, and thrice a week Father Andrade played the organ at their church. He had learned to play the piano as a boy from his uncle, who in his youth had traveled with the Familia Nievesverdes Circus. Father Andrade had also heard his first Bible story from this uncle, who explained to him the books of the Bible and the different authors, their lives, and how their voices together try to harness the One Voice. Later on, when he learned Braille, the books available to him were mostly the classics: Virgil, Shakespeare, Herman Melville, Sappho. Father Andrade read everything he could, and memorized various passages from Aesop, Chaucer, and Edward Lear nonsense that gave him a chuckle.

His way of dressing reminded me of gamblers from my grandfather's generation in Mexico. He wore shaded reading glasses, and I never got to see what his eyes looked like.

Thinking about it now, I'm proud to have formed a friendship with a man like Father Andrade, though at the time I was drinking too much and took it for granted. I wrote everything using a typewriter, with my front door open, so sometimes when he heard the machine he'd come over. I'd stop writing, relieved, and invite him in every time.

I tape-recorded a lot of conversations I had in that efficiency, and many of these were with Father Andrade. After watching *Preying on the Holy*, I told myself I needed those cassettes back, and knew just what had to be done to retrieve them.

I borrowed my boss's car and drove five hours southwest to Atascosa, where my old roommate from the east side, Sally, lived. Neither of us held a grudge over our failed relationship and subsequent falling out. She invited me in for barley soup with her husband, Elian, then brought out a milk crate with things from the old days that weren't hers. There were seven 120-minute cassettes in there, and in my excitement I asked Sally if she'd seen *Preying on the Holy*—she hadn't, and I told her it was fucked-up, highly recommended. When I grabbed the cassettes and started my thank-yous and good-byes, Sally and Elian commented on the immense amount of time we have in life and proposed a threesome. I politely declined, got back in the boss's car, and peeled out of there. I popped an unmarked cassette in the tape deck, screwed with the controls on the stereo, then immediately heard my own voice—and, like it always does, it gave me a sense of dread to hear what I actually sound like.

I took that cassette out and shoved another in, thinking how surreal everything back there with Sally and her husband had been, and I wondered if my decision about the threesome had been the correct one. I heard a parrot and soft jazz playing in a distant room, then footsteps and a montage of various squeaky doors closing. I flipped the cassette over, and it was suddenly the sounds of drunken people talking at some party. Played another cassette, and again my own voice—I seemed to be reciting something—and I turned up the volume as the accordion sun started to set. I sped the tape up, played, and I was still reciting, then I listened to the words—it wasn't my voice but Father Andrade's, reciting Homer, the Fitzgerald translation.

Listening to how clumsily and naively I spoke of literature

embarrassed me. When I got home I finally found the anecdote that had started all this. I'm transcribing it here, verbatim, from the moment I began recording it, and Father Andrade is already in conversation:

. . . had much talent and disappeared in long stretches. For a period I was taken care of by the state, then by the Sala Sagrada nuns. I digress in telling you more than this story needs of my uncle, but after the last time my uncle left, I started to be looked after by a nun from Argentina, Santa Juanita Espada. Never knew how old she was, but I can hear her voice; it feels like the texture of construction paper, always, to this day. I was in her care starting at fifteen. Santa Juanita came from an industrious family that, in the years since she'd left Argentina, had prospered. I think it was a sister of hers that died, and there was a small inheritance that had been wired to Phoenix, Arizona, through some confusion. We were living together in an apartment in San Antonio when she explained we must take a bus trip to Phoenix. Now, I'd never been outside of Texas, and this excited me, to go to another state, and I remembered being fond of the word "Phoenix" from my uncle's stories. See, I had a great curiosity and imagination. I thought magical things could happen at any moment in a city named Phoenix. When we got there it was in the extreme heat, and they gave Santa Juanita some forms to sign. On the ride back to San Antonio the bus broke down. In the middle of the day and in the desert. All of us got off the bus with that fruit-gone-bad radiator smell, and later I heard another car pull over. The bus driver asks the couple in the car where they're going and they say Texas. The only ones going that far in the bus were me and Santa Juanita. The couple in the car offer to take the nun and the blind boy while the others wait for a mechanic. Here we are, the story of this couple. They were named Panchofire and Marina. Pancho like Pancho Villa, and fire like that which burns. Marina, I've always liked that name. Makes you think of the way poets described the sea in the old days. Santa Juanita didn't speak much English and the couple didn't speak a lot of Spanish, though I could tell they were Mexicanos from out west. Santa Juanita was prone to falling asleep in vehicles, and I must say I felt good inside that fast car with those young people. They whispered to each other and were nice enough to talk to me. Especially the girl. When I asked what kind of plans they had in Texas, Panchofire told me he didn't know why he'd lied to the bus driver and said that they were heading to Texas, when they were really going to Tulsa. "Do you want to know why Tulsa?" he asked me. I couldn't think of anything, and he said it was because often people are chosen to right wrongs. And after some silence, he and Marina whispered for a long while, then Panchofire asked if I'd ever heard of a nurse from Texas who was killed on Ash Wednesday, and how her killer had never been caught. I said no, then he asked if I knew why the killer was never caught. When I said I didn't, he said, "Guess." I couldn't guess, of course, and was starting to get scared. I was still a nervous, naive young man in that back seat. Then Marina said it didn't matter. That they were gonna visit the priest who'd last seen her, who'd crossed the ashes on her forehead the last night she was alive. Crossed the ashes. On her forehead. Me and Santa Juanita got back to San Antonio that evening and honestly haven't thought of that couple, Panchofire and Marina, in a long time. Something in the radiator smell of the wind tonight, I suppose, just reminded me.

EL RITMO DE LA NOCHE

El Ritmo de la Noche was not so much a rhythm—although that's still debated—but a salsa, its initial distribution traced back to two high school dropouts from the Valley. One of them, Octavio H., was sleeping through his sophomore English II class, and he audibly gasped when the teacher banged on his desk to awaken him. When Octavio's eyes dilated to his peers laughing at his expense, he got up and said, "This class is nothing, I don't need to be here. 'Cause you know what? I make the money. I go fishing at the canal and then sell the fish to the store. I don't need any of this." He walked out the door as the teacher watched with her arms crossed. There had previously been problems with Octavio, and since in those days the campus was open, she let him go as he pleased.

Octavio wandered out of the school, past the graveyard, through the wheat field, until he ended up in front of a junked-out Rolls-Royce with many chile trees growing through and around it. Hunched over the driver's seat, picking chiles from the branch going through the rear window and dropping them into a pail, was Octavio's friend and business partner, Alex Z. Octavio leaned on the open door and whistled shrilly. Alex jumped back, startled, and honked the horn with his ass. They both laughed, shut the door to the Rolls-Royce, and made their way toward the trailer of the woman they called the Astronaut, due to the old space helmet she kept among potted plants on her mosquito-netted front porch.

Upon the boys' arrival, the Astronaut was already waiting with a large Styrofoam ice chest. She took the pail of chiles from Alex, pointed at the chest, and the two boys opened it. Many jars were stacked inside, and steam rose from the bottom because their contents were hot. On every jar was a white label with the words EL RITMO DE LA NOCHE, between two shoddily Sharpied musical notes that resembled hockey sticks. Alex and Octavio loaded the Styrofoam ice chest onto a rusty wheelbarrow and took turns pushing it until shortly before dusk, when they arrived at the club Pasito Tun-Tun. The manager, Roel, was expecting the boys, and two young men only a few years older than Octavio and Alex took the chest from the wheelbarrow and carried it out back.

Roel, with grave concern, asked the boys about the Astronaut—how her health seemed. The boys looked at each other and agreed that she appeared fine. Roel nodded, gave them each a sealed envelope and a free shot of the strong stuff, then excused himself—he had a club to run, he said.

Octavio and Alex opened their envelopes about fifty feet

from the club and counted the money. "I'd make more sticking to my fish," Octavio said. "And it's less work." They agreed to team up again either way, and before parting set a time to meet the following morning at the junked-out Rolls-Royce.

Back at the club, in the manager's office, Roel smoked a cigarette as he stared into the open ice chest. He picked up a jar, and with his right thumb traced the hockey stick musical notes. "El Ritmo de la Noche," he said to himself. Saying the words aloud brought a mysterious breeze into the closed room, as if he'd read them from a sacred book. He put out his cigarette and sealed the chest, then instructed the two young men on his payroll to wrap the chest carefully in trash bags and carry it to his truck, which was loaded with other similar packages. Roel didn't trust anybody to make this shipment, so he took a shot of the same stuff he'd given the boys, then drove the truck north himself.

He made it past customs without a problem, and in the town of Fal met up with his man in an uninhabited mauve shack. His man inspected El Ritmo de la Noche, really taking his time with it. Finally, as if coming to this conclusion reluctantly, his man said he could probably extract a good dance number out of it. Maybe even a hit single.

So it was agreed, and there in that mauve shack they opened every jar of El Ritmo de la Noche and boiled the contents down, trapped the vapors, and stored them in vials. Roel then paid his man, and moved the vials not only down south and farther north, but to every major city in the tristate area. Soon, El Ritmo de la Noche was the big hit of the summer, then of the year. It was played on every hip station and spun in every club; people danced to El Ritmo de la Noche in the streets. Nobody could believe this hit, and when the royalties came in, neither could Roel, who had to admit he'd scored big.

Years went by, then decades, and Roel felt he'd put old properties, marriages, and politicians behind him—after everything, he was grateful that investments like El Ritmo de la Noche were still paying off. One evening, he was reflecting on his early nightclub days, as he stared at an empty jar he hadn't seen in a long time. It had a white label with hockey stick musical notes, and had recently been sent to him with a little message inside, requesting a meeting.

Moments later, Roel's head butler appeared in the office studio and announced, "Sir, your guest has arrived." Roel got up from his puffy leather chair and greeted the stout, balding man entering his office. "So it is you, Octavio. We meet again."

The following afternoon, after finding it odd that Roel hadn't come down all morning, the head butler found him dead, slumped over his leather chair in the office studio. When questioned by medics and the police, the head butler told them the last time he'd seen Roel alive was when he'd brought the balding man into his office. The head butler couldn't recall the balding man's name, and hadn't caught him leaving, but mentioned the peculiar jar labeled EL RITMO DE LA NOCHE they'd received anonymously only days prior. There didn't appear to be foul play, and it was later determined that Roel had suffered a heart attack. When the head butler and the police officers looked for the jar labeled EL RITMO DE LA NOCHE in the office studio, it was nowhere to be found.

YOU GOT IT, TAKE IT AWAY

After talking to my father for over an hour—the dialogue meandering, banal, almost entirely one-sided—he passingly mentioned that my aunt and uncle had been crashing with him. My father lived in a small trailer with many problems, inside a community of people fifty-five and older, so I found this news—which he'd muttered effortlessly, like using a horsehair as a brush to add a tiny detail to a painting—disturbing.

"No te preocupes," he told me; then in English, for flair, he added: "Don't worry about it," with the inflection of a movie gangster.

I pressed him for details, but he was vague. Before ending the conversation he said, as if I'd wrung it out of him, "Pues así están las cosas," then asked if I'd be watching the ball game. He urged me not to stay indoors all the time, to go get drunk at a bar and watch the World Series.

I told him that's what my problem had been for many years, getting drunk at bars, which is why I stayed home now, but he didn't find it as funny as I'd thought he would.

I ended up going to the old bar, caught some of the game, but was disappointed the jukebox was gone. They'd replaced it with one of those digital things that charge two dollars a song, but you could play any song—any song, eh?

I left the bar two beers in, unable to think of a single song I wanted to hear for two dollars. That night my neighbor was sitting outside his end of the duplex—from a little radio he played loud Cuban music, though he was white and understood no Spanish.

"Raf," he said, "I've been noticing your style. You always carry a big book. Surely you read them, too? Or are they just for self-defense? Kids around here, you know, don't read."

Lewis—my neighbor—was tipsy, possibly drunk. I recognized remnants of shooting insulin on a small tray next to him, and thought he must be diabetic, so drinking couldn't be good for him.

Up in the sky was one of those moons that was supposed to be something special—like a blood moon, or solstice one—but it just looked like a regular spiderweb moon to me. I wanted to get around Lewis as fast as possible, but he raised an arm as if flagging me down and said, "Raf, I'm going to tell it to you straight. I don't have long to live. I've done what I could for myself here, and with the money I make, my hospital bills, and rent, the future can't be good. No way José I'm ever moving again, either—"

The "no way José" did it and I started walking past him. "Please. I want to show you something," he said, in a pleading tone that persuaded me.

"I have beers in the fridge. I'll grab you one," he offered, and winked.

In a flash I envisioned my dying days as an old man, just needing to talk to somebody after some beers. So I followed him in, even though I knew Lewis was a jerk, and more than likely incorrigibly racist. Plus, I hadn't thought to pick up any beer, and now I could keep my buzz going.

"I don't recall mentioning it before," he said, "but my family is from New Mexico. New Mexico has an abnormal relationship with the sky, as you've probably heard."

There are blues songs about living in a room so small it resembles a matchbox—and though our apartments were the same size, Lewis's side managed to look just like that, with stacked shelves and tables of hoarded newspapers, VHS tapes, and tabloid magazines.

Clippings about bank robberies and boxing matches and oil spills adorned various parts of the walls. Lewis brought out a small framed photograph of a young woman and a wide-eyed man in a fancy suit.

"That's my ma, with Harry Houdini," he said.

I don't know why, but I laughed. This put Lewis off. He hastily hid the photo, frowning, and I feared I'd killed this moment. Lewis and I had been duplex neighbors for over two years. Apart from the time we got together to complain to the landlords about the plumbing, we had never exchanged more than a few sentences. We'd definitely never entered each other's homes.

I heard sounds of rummaging coming from his bedroom. Neither of us talked for a good few minutes, and he must have turned off the radio, because the Cuban music that'd been so inviting was gone.

Lewis came out carrying an unmarked, smooth wooden box, with two hasps he thumbed to unlatch.

"People talk about Roswell like it's the only big thing," he said. Lewis opened the box, took out a thin gray fabric that rippled like liquid. It appeared both metallic and made of cloth. Lewis held it out and gestured in such a way that I knew he wanted me to feel it with my fingers. The material was cool, like finely woven chain mail, the way I always imagined chain mail to be in Arthurian sagas.

The fabric was just bigger than a handkerchief, and as Lewis held it by two corners, the material continued to ripple like the surface of a pond in thin air.

"What is it?"

Lewis put his left hand through the middle of the cloth. The cloth wrapped itself around his fingers and acted like an elbow-length glove. He extended his arm, showing how tightly the fabric was wrapped, as if it were fit for him exclusively. It made his hand both shiny and transparent, depending on the angle.

Lewis said, "My old man. He was in the Air Force. His

job one day was to go out and help recover a bad wreckage. Out in the desert."

"Like aliens? Real aliens, from outer space?"

Lewis replied, "My old man. He took what he knew to the grave. We ended up finding this in a box after he passed."

Lewis crumpled the cloth, tossed it to the ground, and it bounced like a tennis ball toward me, which I wasn't expecting, and I nearly didn't catch it. The ball turned back into a liquid, gray cloth in my hands. Its texture was thin, nearly see-through—but if I tried to shape it, the material behaved more like aluminum foil. I folded it first into a cube, then a pyramid, and placed it on a newspaper stack on the coffee table, admiring its sturdiness. Then, when I reached to grab it, the cloth seemed to anticipate this and went limp, back to its original texture. When held close to a light source, it disappeared like smoke—when held away again, it lost its camouflage.

I folded it into an airplane, in a way I hadn't done since I was a boy, and launched it over to Lewis. The cloth glided like the lightest papier-mâché.

Lewis finally handed me a beer, put the cloth back in the wooden box, and talked about his family and military service, without telling me more about the cloth. I knew the subject was long gone when he went on a rant about his disdain for Texas and Texans, then, to prove it further, he started singing a song about the sweetness of Oklahoma.

As I got up to leave, Lewis looked at me with bloodshot eyes and said, "Bandannas like those are what you wish. What you wish you and your homies could wear."

Finding the comment more strange than insulting, I left him to his matchbox side of the duplex.

Meanwhile, my electricity bill hadn't been paid in seven months. I'd received my final notice, did what everyone advised and called to get on a payment plan, though I knew that would accomplish little in getting the bill paid. But it kept the lights on temporarily and that's what mattered.

Between the hustle of home and work, biking, riding the bus, and even when I'd wake up in the middle of the night, I couldn't help but have one thing return to my mind: the liquid cloth belonging to Lewis. Once, taking a cigarette break during my shift, I caught myself pantomiming slipping the cloth on like a glove, in the same manner I'd seen Lewis do. I'd also called my father only once during this time, and he was as chaotic and vague as ever about the state of his own affairs.

On my next day off I made the decisions to stay sober and to knock on Lewis's door. I'd been thinking of the last thing he'd said to me before I left his place. His Chevy was parked in his driveway and was filthy with bird shit and leaves—like he hadn't driven it for days. I knocked again and said, "Lewis, it's me—Rafael, your neighbor. You okay in there?"

"Come in," he yelled.

Lewis was watching a reality show on a tiny television

that sat on a stack of tabloid magazines on the coffee table. He was reclined on one side of his couch, and had his right foot elevated at the opposite end, as if it pained him.

"My neighbor," he said, "from down south of the border."

Lewis's eyes looked redder than ever behind his small, rectangular glasses. I saw his balding, scabbed head in the evening light coming in through the kitchen window. I looked around for signs that he'd been drinking but didn't see any bottles or cans anywhere. His place was more piled than before with *TV Guides*, completed crossword puzzle books, and gun magazines going back to the eighties.

"I'm from south of the border, but a citizen in this country now, Lewis. I can vote and I have the same rights as you or any other fellow American."

This made Lewis chuckle. I sensed he was feeling mean.

Preempting whatever response he might have had as he pointed one finger at me, I said, "Lewis, remember when you had me over a few weeks ago, and—"

"You were inside my house?"

"I mean. Yes."

"How'd you get in?"

"You invited me in, Lewis, c'mon. You showed me your father's cloth and everything."

Lewis propped himself up, and his attitude became less menacing, more alert, perhaps cautious. "I don't know what you're talking about," he said.

A rush was going through me, and I got the same feeling I get when arguing with my GM at work. Lewis had been a displeasing presence in my life since I'd become his neighbor, and within a few weeks of living here I had seen that he resented the people living around him. Many times he'd called the police on the teenagers in the apartment complex next door who blared their hip-hop in the parking lot, and I'd heard other stories that'd given me pause. In short, Lewis had been on and off my shit list for the past couple years. But I had also learned that Lewis had severe medical problems, not only from diabetes, but also from complications after his ex-wife shot him and blew one kidney out. Though none of the neighbors knew the details of this incident, everyone unanimously, without asking, agreed Lewis must've done something to deserve it.

"All right, Lewis," I said, trying not to stutter. "You had good music playing and invited me in, showed me pics of your ma and Houdini, showed off this cloth material, being all shady, telling me it's from outer space and all that—"

"I oughta call the police on you. For going through my stuff. Get out of my house."

"Okay, I'll get out. I'll never come back here, either. But last time when I left you told me something, Lewis. You said how I probably wished that cloth you showed me would be the bandanna me and my homies could wear. I just want to point out that you live around many different types of brown and Black folks here. Almost never do you see any of us wearing a bandanna. How about that?"

"Get out of here," Lewis said. He reached for a crutch and got up. I was curious to see what he'd do, so I didn't move. It was obvious Lewis was in bad shape.

He opened a drawer under his old radio, and, as if exerting a great amount of strength, pulled out a red baseball cap. Grinning, he dropped back down onto the couch and put the cap with those four white embroidered words on his head.

I would have respected Lewis's wishes the first time he told me to get out, but I sensed he was enjoying the tension, and now I knew why. This was his punch line.

The front door had been open this entire time, and he said, "You're letting the flies in."

"Whatever, Lewis. But I want you to know something. That I took an oath in a room with close to a thousand other people to defend the United States Constitution and the founding principles of this country—"

"Bullshit," he exclaimed. "I was born in this country, never had to take no oath."

"That's exactly right. You've never had to study the details of this country and what it supposedly stands for, and then had to take an oral exam about it—as an adult. Do you know how many people in Congress there even are?"

"Over four hundred."

"Who are our senators?"

He told me.

"What was the cause of the Civil War?"

He was about to reply, then stopped himself, grinned, and pointed a finger at me again, this time in a *you almost got me there* kinda way.

"Anyway, this is where I'm getting at, Lewis. We have a sworn loyalty to this country, which in the end belongs to the people. You have that cloth made out of that fucked-up material you said your father supposedly recovered from an alien spacecraft. And if you have information about it, then you need to come out with it. Because the people need to know."

Lewis was just staring at me from under that red cap. Even I was surprised by what I'd said. Upon knocking on his door, I hadn't imagined we'd come this far, flinging around words like "spacecraft," "constitution," and "oath."

Then, on a whim—why not?—I took a risk, and said: "Give the cloth over to me, Lewis. I'll keep it in the box and keep it safe. You don't have any children, any heirs. I'll make sure it gets into safe hands. Like we're cowboys in a western and the frontier is all ours, and I'm making a promise to you on your deathbed. It's one of those things like why we have the words 'faith' and 'honor,' and those beautiful stringed instruments are playing in the background in this scene. Please, just give the cloth over to me, Lewis. You can trust me that your great legacy will live on."

In a voice that became deeper, lower, so that I knew he meant it, Lewis said: "Get the hell out of my household."

It took all my energy to not throw him the finger as I walked back to my side of the duplex, where I blared old-school hip-hop, making sure it reverberated all the way through the walls.

Since that exchange with Lewis, I made a point to enter the courtyard of our duplex through the back alley, in order to avoid his door at the main entrance. Having bad blood with anyone doesn't sit well with me; my instincts are always to reach out to the other person and try to make things right. In this case, however, I could see that nothing would ever get resolved by reaching out. Lewis was the person he was, and he seemed to work hard at maintaining that persona. I didn't have to befriend everyone in my life, even within the cheap places a lot of us are forced to live, close to one another, whether we like it or not.

What I did resent, however, was him keeping this liquid cloth to himself. Why should he hoard all that power? And what could this cloth actually be? I used various search engines and skimmed through every nonfiction book about Roswell and spacecraft wreckages I could find at the public library with no success, until terms like "alien autopsy" and "Hynek's scale" became part of my vernacular and I started freaking my coworkers out.

I considered sharing all this with my father, since neighbor feuds and the supernatural were subjects he could relate to, but I never brought it up.

He did, however, fill me in on what had been going on, and his reasons for being so ambiguous about my aunt and uncle. It was no big secret within my family that my aunt and uncle had been in the country without papers as far back as my childhood. So when he told me they were crashing with him, I could only imagine the reasons.

In recent years, even their most loyal previous employers had stopped giving them work, in large part due to the political climate. Horror stories had been circulating of workplace deportations. My aunt and uncle started talking about moving back to Mexico, and after a long deliberation, with support from the rest of the family, they'd sold their property and had been crashing with my father for just over a month as they made arrangements.

When I asked my father how he felt about sheltering them, he painted it as somewhat emotionally taxing, but ultimately no big deal. "They're over there now. We all played our part in what had to be done," he told me. He laughed, then said, "It's like the película, con el 'You got it, take it away.'"

"Cual película?" I said. "Which movie? That's from Johnny Canales's show."

Johnny Canales was the host of *The Johnny Canales Show*, a variety show that aired every Sunday in South Texas, famous during the eighties and nineties for showcasing Tejano and conjunto bands from Mexican communities around the country, and one of the first television programs to have Selena y Los Dinos perform. Canales sat behind a desk, not unlike Johnny Carson, but wearing his trademark large glasses and flashy suits. "You got it, take it away" was his catchphrase—I couldn't remember if he said it before cutting to commercials, after introducing an artist, at the end of his show, or all three. Growing up, Johnny Canales was always something of a joke between me and my grungy friends, but now as an adult I can see what an icon the man was.

"*No'mbre, cual* Johnny Canales," my father said. "Es el Bogart, the actor in that movie. The woman who he was in love with comes back into his life asking him for help many years after he last saw her. Remember? The Nazis were after the man she had married. You know Bogart wishes things were different and he could be together with her. But her husband needs papers to leave or they'll be dead. Bogart gets his underground connections, even hoodlums he doesn't know very well, to do their part in helping them leave before World War II. *Ya*, when they're on the plane, Bogart turns to his friend, surely before going to get some beers to celebrate, *y le dice*: 'Amigo, you got it, take it away.'"

I was thoroughly entertained by this take and didn't bother further contradicting my father's memory. The more I thought about it, the more marvelous it became, and the more I laughed. My father had somehow conflated Johnny Canales's catchphrase with the last line of *Casablanca*. I really, really wished for him to be right. For weeks after that phone call, during random moments, I'd picture Johnny Canales in glorious black and white, wearing that long trench coat and hat Bogart is famous for in *Casablanca*, emerging from the fog holding a pistol, ready to shoot a fascist.

It'd been years since I'd watched the movie, so I borrowed a small TV with a built-in VHS player, and rented it from the last video store in town. After I watched the movie, it became clearer than ever: Johnny Canales as the owner of the Blue Parrot, drowning his sorrows as he watches the tourists drink and gamble while all hell breaks loose around the world; Johnny Canales reading that farewell letter in the heartbreaking rain; Johnny Canales, in what he knows is possibly his last chance, holding Ingrid Bergman, and really looking into her eyes to say those famous words.

I watched it while spending Christmas Day alone, and this last image of Johnny Canales is what did it for me. This impossible idea of a silver-screen legend like Ingrid Bergman having this doomed love affair with Johnny Canales, a Spanglish-speaking border ranchero turned Tejano, who styled himself and talked like any one of my uncles, was just too unbearable. It even made me remember my own lost loves and dead family members. With all the lights in my apartment off, I had one of those good, heaving cries, where your insides tumble out and you don't know who you are anymore.

Boxing Day: a holiday we don't observe in America, though I always thought it was the perfect way to describe a Christmas hangover. I decided to take a walk around the east side and find coffee, thinking of my aunt and my uncle and my father. Again, I couldn't help admiring how my father's immigrant memory juxtaposed those two bits of American pop culture. Even when I was young and ignorant about cinema, I knew that the last line of *Casablanca*—the real last line—was a cultural phenomenon within itself: "Louis, I think this is the beginning of a beautiful friendship." Spoken to an almost stranger, of course, after learning that they could make a few bucks on the side while fighting fascists. It's the last line you'd wish for in the biopic of your own life, scheming as you walked away into the credits.

When I headed back to the duplex, I noticed a commotion coming from Lewis's place. There was a moving truck, and two young men were carrying stuff out of the apartment; a trash bin sat on the curb brimming with the glossy magazines and old furniture I had seen in Lewis's place.

The palms of my hands started sweating as I deliberated for a second about rushing in there to find that wooden box with the liquid cloth—that gray, sweet metallic cloth I could never forget.

A group of kids was gathered in the parking lot across the street, blaring music, watching the men emptying Lewis's place. One of them was the kid with the red Mohawk whom I'd bought raffle tickets from before.

"This guy finally moved out?" I said to the kid.

Another kid, sitting next to an upside-down BMX bike, said, "Nah, he died."

"What?"

"The ambulance took his body the other day," the kid with the red Mohawk said.

"No way."

All the kids nodded. Though Lewis was in many ways the neighborhood antagonist, and it was the day after Christmas, they were all quite somber and displeased.

Much later, I found out through the landlords that Lewis had suffered a heart attack from a gangrene infection in his foot that had spread in part because of his diabetes. It turned out he did have two sons he rarely talked to, and it was the two of them who were clearing out his apartment.

That day, standing next to the kids blasting their mixtapes, it wasn't lost on me how close Lewis's name was to the name in the real last line of *Casablanca*. Lewis's sons never acknowledged us, didn't make eye contact even once, as they loaded the truck.

I looked at the kids and said, "You got it, take it away," with behind-the-desk gestures and all—but there's no way they could have gotten the reference.

Passing the courtyard entrance, I established my presence enough that both brothers made eye contact with me, and I gave them a sympathetic nod. When I decided to take a longer stroll, I walked by my apartment, slipped through the alley. Without looking back, as the kids zoomed along the streets on their bikes, I said, loud enough for anybody to hear, "Lewis, I think this is the beginning of a beautiful friendship."

PHEASANTS

FOR RANDY "BISCUIT" TURNER

Three days after the rent was due, Renata Three and Tito Papel spread their money out on the rug. They shared a bottle of André as Tito Papel counted, then Renata Three counted it again, then together they counted a few more times to be sure. After a moment of deep concern, they figured if they were already $180 short, another $20 or $30 wasn't going to hurt, so they decided on going out to meet their friends downtown after all.

The next morning, taking the trash out in the middle of the double she was working, Tito Papel saw the feathered angel. The feathered angel sat on a log with their wings tucked, eating a chunk of birthday cake somebody had thrown away and that they'd fished out of the trash, no doubt.

"All right," Tito said. "First of all," and she pointed at the feathered angel's cheeks and chin, "you're getting it all over your face. Your feathers and shit."

"Whoops. My bad, sergeant. I'll find a river somewhere and dunk my head in."

Tito saw the feathered angel really chow down on the cake in a way she hadn't seen someone do since she was small, like at a kid's birthday party, where none of the children knew yet how to eat cake without getting it on themselves.

Artists have notions of angels, thinking that they look like people—Tito Papel had thought this many times, and in many ways this depiction of them is true—but what they never get right is their skin, with their tiny feathers, which bring to mind tall, beakless birds. Tito watched the way the tiny feathers around the angel's mouth fluttered and acted as a natural napkin, cleaning their face of the old, tepid orange icing.

"All right," Tito said. "That's enough of this. Look, my boss can come out here anytime and kick you out again. Is that what you want? It'll just embarrass both of us."

"Oh, come on, Tito, you and me are cool now. I brought you that bottle of Jamaican rum last time."

"And that was very nice of you, but I also have to say that was the right thing for you to do. I'm not gonna give you props for doing the right thing here—"

"Come on—"

"Look—you coming out here, eating our trash, interrogating us at work. This is an insult."

The feathered angel set the melting cake aside.

"How am I insulting you?" they asked.

"I mean, you follow a different divine social order than

me, my coworkers, our girlfriends. Even a higher order than the prettiest face in this world. I'm working a double today, hungover as hell because I'm short on the rent—plus the late fee. Meanwhile, you're all up there in the clouds flying in the sky and shit. You don't gotta pay rent to nobody. Yet here you are, messing with us, picking through our trash—"

The feathered angel gave up and said, "I see it your way now. I don't know why I like to eat this stuff. I can't even taste anything. Then again, I don't even have the concept you do when I use the word 'I.' Nevertheless, I use this clunky language to communicate with you."

"All right," said Tito. "You don't have to shame me for using this inferior language to talk. I gotta go back to work now, lunch rush's almost up, and I'm gonna come back out here for a toke, so. Please be gone?"

Tito Papel and Renata Three made it through autumn more or less making the rent the same way together, then after the holidays they decided to break up. But not before one more night of smashing disco balls, eating leg of mutton, and fucking—then they went their separate ways.

Tito had picked up a couple double shifts a week while looking for a roommate. During a toke break before her shift one cold day, Tito saw the feathered angel in the alley again, sitting on a milk crate, wings peeking out from their shoulders, not eating trash or anything disgusting this time.

"What kind of work do you do here, anyway? Eres bode-guero?" they asked in Spanish.

Tito replied, "Bodeguero? Like a warehouse worker? Or like in the northeastern sense?"

"Like, is this a little bodega you work in?"

"Bodega? Are you from the fucking Bronx? News flash: a bodega is just a regular-ass convenience store where they can make you a sandwich. Right? Calm down with your bodega talk, buddy. Do you know where you even are? You are in Texas."

"I know where I am," said the feathered angel. "You know, the word 'Texas,' what it means? 'Friend.'"

"Well, it should probably mean 'absolute, crushing defeat.' You wanna know another bit of useless knowledge? The French word 'château' means 'girl.' But, say, friend—you're flying around, can you see anyone out there who is reliable and needs a place to live? I'm in deep need of a roommate."

"Excuse me? What in good grace do you think I am here?"

"Well, I don't know, you're my guardian angel, no? Hovering around me at work—"

"Whoa, whoa. Guardian angel? Is that what you think I am, sergeant? An angel watching over you? Making sure you don't screw up at every step?"

"I mean, I'm not saying you're doing a bad job. Or necessarily that you're even *my* guardian angel, but certainly somebody's? And why wouldn't you be useful like that to someone?"

"This may come as a regrettable surprise, but there's something you need to know. The inherent egotism of your kind prevents you from seeing something: that the existence of my kind, or of any living creature here, is not necessarily contingent on your own."

"What the hell does that mean? Use people words—"

"You think my kind—and I use the term 'my kind' because it's something you can understand; to use the true name of our kind would split your skull in half—exists for the benefit of your own? Like, we're out here watching you and knowing everyone's lunches and fates and such? That's the egotism of your kind, friend. Thinking there's living beings existing just for the benefit of your existence. I cannot feel being baffled, but I do believe that 'baffle' is a word that can be used to describe this—"

"Okay, I get it. I've had enough now. Going back to work. You win this round, feathered angel. You know, I've told people about you. I've even told all my friends back home about you. And you know what? It's actually astonishing. Nobody gives a fuck. At most, they'll say, 'Oh, yeah, a feathered angel? Cool,' and then look at you like you're probably trying to prove you're hot shit back in the city. But really you're just talking about your life back here. Anyway, that's all I got. Peace."

Through a clever ad she uploaded, Tito Papel found a roommate, Liz, and celebrated by taking a few days off work and buying new pants and sneakers. Increasingly, she paid attention to the dog shadows that appeared around her day and night, but rarely did she see a dog casting them.

Summer was almost over, and with a combination of wishful thinking, hustling, and luck, Tito Papel leveled out financially, though she was still always broke.

On her penultimate shift at the coffee shop, while taking out the trash and having a smoke, Tito Papel heard a sound she didn't think was from this earth—and in a way she was right, because there behind the bare-branched linden tree was the feathered angel, hunched over and retching.

Before asking them anything, Tito noticed the tiny feathers around their face rippling with each facial contortion, and the rainbow puke on the ground before them.

Tito said, "Jesus, are you okay?"

"All good," the feathered angel said, between retching and heaving. "Just fell a little ill, that's all."

"Ill? Aren't you a divine being? How are you sick?"

"I don't know, sergeant. Maybe something I ate."

"I bet."

The wings on their back went taut, then fluttered when the puke came, this time in blue and yellow, and Tito stepped back.

"What kind of angel are you to get sick? Did you eat trash again?"

"What's trash? The stuff in these bags, you mean? The ones you're throwing out?"

"Yes, that's garbage, and it's bad. You shouldn't be eating it; that's like a basic rule here on earth. I could get you some Pepto, but I'm not sure that would work with what you got."

Tito gazed at the puddle of green, blue, and orange oils the feathered angel had puked up, and said, "'On earth as it is in heaven'—I guess I understand now."

The feathered angel shook as if they had been taken ahold of by a viper fever, and genuflected. Tito Papel held their hand and glared at the puddle of puke, which didn't have an odor. She wondered what kind of song a musician could write from this. She thought of the devil, and how the devil is often depicted as a businessperson wanting to make the ultimate capitalist deal. When angels approach us— maybe—they are troubled beings themselves, like alcoholic old mates looking to make amends. And a goddess? How would a goddess approach us?

Months later, Tito Papel chose to skip going back home for Thanksgiving—she'd been invited by a coworker for a "Friendsgiving" kind of thing with a bunch of strangers, and though she'd been inclined not to go, at the last minute she changed her mind.

Upon arrival, Tito Papel was surprised to see Renata Three—and it took reassurances from their host to get over the initial awkwardness upon learning they were exes. Tito Papel saw how she and Renata Three had both changed— they weren't the kind of people to be too late on the rent anymore. After a few glasses of wine, and pheasant as the main course instead of turkey, Renata Three asked about the feathered angel—if Tito Papel still ran into them.

When Tito Papel responded, "Yes. Just the other day I saw the feathered angel puking their guts out in an alley," Renata Three laughed—mostly because maybe she missed Tito, just a little.

THE OSWALD VARIATIONS

1.

He's better known as the man who assassinated JFK, but a few still remember Lee Harvey as the front man in the two lost recordings of the band Sarcophagus. Lee Harvey's brief musical career began shortly after he got discharged from the Marines and moved into the attic room of his mother's apartment, off Hemlock Avenue, on the east side of Dallas. Lee Harvey's only belongings during this time were a duffel bag stuffed with clothes; a cheap phonograph, on which he played Shostakovich, blues recorded at Angola State Prison, and Johnnie Ray's hit singles; Bertolt Brecht and Karel Čapek's plays in paperback; a shoddy hardcover of Olaf Stapledon's *Last and First Men*; and three framed photographs. One was of Lee Harvey's mother holding him as a baby boy, another was an image of Madame Blavatsky he'd cut out of *Life* magazine, and the third was of an unidentified vaudevillian actress from the late nineteenth century, which was the only portrait he kept out of sight.

2. In which Lee Harvey makes a friend and talks radical ideas on art.

3. In which Lee Harvey is let in on a secret after work.

2. In which Lee Harvey makes a friend and talks radical ideas on art.

Lee Harvey got hired as an apprentice at Strauss-McNeely Books & Binding, where he was to learn the art of collating academic monographs. It was here that he struck up a friendship with another employee, Sinclair Bowling, after Lee Harvey identified a tune the young Okie was whistling as a piece by Mussorgsky. The two young men tossed around the names of other composers and works of literature during lunchtime and over the course of the workday. Lee Harvey listened attentively to Bowling's ideas about Russian constructivism in the context of postwar America, and in turn Bowling listened to Lee Harvey's stance on what's been going wrong with southwestern musical ideals since 1917. After their shift one day, they caught the same bus back to East Dallas and discussed Hart Crane, though Lee Harvey was familiar mostly with the man's final days and suicide rather than his poetry.

4. Lee Harvey, on an inspired whim, buys a guitar.

5. A pessimistic Lee Harvey has a sinister vision involving colors.

3. In which Lee Harvey is let in on a secret after work.

It was at Strauss-McNeely Books & Binding that Lee Harvey was hired to learn the art of collating academic monographs, and where he made friends with another employee, Sinclair Bowling. They were both going opposite ways in the stairwell when a paperback book fell out of Lee Harvey's pocket. As Sinclair Bowling picked it up and handed it to Lee Harvey, he saw it was a copy of *An Illustrated Anthology of Maritime Disasters* by L. M. Morick. The young men then discussed events like the sinking of the *Pride of La Goncourt*, the fire on the *General Slocum*, and the torpedoing of the famous *Lusitania*.

During their lunch break the two young men conversed about paintings and visual art. Bowling pontificated that in the future, televisions would be three-dimensional and hover like big soap bubbles in our homes. Lee Harvey said he didn't know what to believe about the future of our homes.

After their shift, Sinclair Bowling decided he could be friends with a guy like Lee Harvey, and let him in on a secret.

They walked two blocks east, to an old blue house where Bowling said a man let him play his piano organ and drink his liquor if he watched his dog.

"He leaves you in his house alone?" asked Lee Harvey.

"Yes."

"And where does he go?"

"I don't know. I think to visit his children."

6. Lee Harvey finds inspiration and trouble.

7. Our protagonist gets inadvertently involved with the Russians, decides to start anew.

4. Lee Harvey, on an inspired whim, buys a guitar.

Toward the end of that fateful bus ride, Bowling casually mentioned being technically proficient with a harmonium; said he could also hold a steady beat on a rudimentary drum kit. Lee Harvey lied and claimed he could strike a few chords on a guitar. That evening, a restless Lee Harvey bought a guitar with a crooked fret board at a secondhand shop, along with a manual for learning chords from the sheet-music store, using his last nine dollars.

8. In which Lee Harvey's work supervisor relates a few things to the Warren Commission.

9. Lee Harvey's mother gives the world a piece of her mind regarding her son.

5. A pessimistic Lee Harvey has a sinister vision involving colors.

Lee Harvey, one day, couldn't bring himself to go to work, and with a gray twinkle in his eye, decided, "None of these earthly things are for me."

He took a bus in the evening to the water tower, climbed the fence and ladder all the way to the top. He smoked a cigarette and stared at the bottle-glass twilight. Lee Harvey envisioned a world where countries were named after colors, and saw himself being a citizen of, and fighting for, a red country. In this country he'd marry a red wife, they'd have red children, and he would vote for a red leader. Naturally, Lee Harvey thought, I'd have to be a red person, too. He thought of other countries with other colors—a blue country taking over an orange country and becoming purple; a green country befriending a yellow one and becoming greener; then all the colors would fight one another and melt into something else—a mysterious color nobody could see coming.

When Lee Harvey climbed down the water tower, the buses were no longer running. He was hungry, but knew it'd take over an hour to walk home. His mother would be sleeping by then. He'd have to take off his shoes and make himself a bologna sandwich really quietly, so as not to wake her.

Yes, Lee Harvey thought, that's what I'll do, and he walked toward home imagining the world as a big, mysterious color.

End.

6. Lee Harvey finds inspiration and trouble.

It was in their third after-work escapade while watching a man named Joe Baca's dog, playing the piano organ, and drinking schnapps, that Lee Harvey spotted a guitar case hiding behind a door. He pulled it out, played a G: it was tuned. Lee Harvey remembered simple chord progressions, and soon enough Sinclair Bowling was able to play along with Lee Harvey. They laughed and saw the whole thing as more of a joke than anything serious.

During their fifth session, while playing a single-note tune that foreshadowed electronic minimalism, Joe Baca stormed into the house and in a loud whisper said to the young men, "I need to hide. If the police arrive, tell them you two are brothers and that you live here. Oh, and your father works as a carpenter."

Lee Harvey and Sinclair Bowling thought Joe Baca was kidding and played for twenty more minutes before they finally went home.

At the bookbindery the next day, they were both fired.

In contrast to Bowling, Lee Harvey was neither surprised nor indignant, and considered the possibility of buying a guitar with his last dollars. They both agreed that their former boss at the bookbindery was a mule, and walked a couple blocks to Joe Baca's house, but when they got there they found it abandoned and all boarded up.

7. Our protagonist gets inadvertently involved with the Russians, decides to start anew.

The man's name was Joe Baca. For five days in the span of two weeks, he let Sinclair Bowling and Lee Harvey Oswald play the piano organ at his house unattended while they watched his dog, and he went off whistling down Chiprock Street.

Sinclair Bowling would sit in front of the keys and go at them while Lee Harvey learned to tune and strum an old guitar Joe Baca kept around.

En route to their sixth venture at the blue house, they found two police vehicles parked at the curb. Three officers and a man in a dark suit approached the young men. The suited man asked Lee Harvey and Sinclair Bowling a couple of questions, and through this Lee and Sinclair discovered that Joe Baca's real name was Alexei Petrovich Antonovich, and that he was an undercover operative for the Soviet Union. Sinclair Bowling, upon hearing the news, spit on the ground and called the officers traitors. Lee Harvey was astonished at his friend's boldness and they both ran away in an intense rush of antiestablishment rebellion.

After a while they both caught their breath and parted ways.

Days passed.

Lee Harvey kept a low profile and became interested in string concertos. One evening he came across the phrase "the human comedy" and couldn't fathom what the real meaning of this phrase could be. He sold all his records and paperback books, fell for the idea that art does not inspire positive change in society, and even dropped the dream of ever owning a guitar. Using most of the money, he bought himself a boat ticket to Europe, then planned to head to Poland, where he knew a person who could get him a Soviet passport.

Lee Harvey wrote a letter to his mother, took a bus out to the harbor in the Gulf alone, and nobody in the United States heard from him for over a year.

End.

8. In which Lee Harvey's work supervisor relates a few things to the Warren Commission.

It is at this point in the story that accounts start to differ significantly and run wild. In the Warren Commission report, Theodore Strauss, immediate supervisor of Lee Harvey and Sinclair Bowling at the bookbindery, said that what the boys discussed at the bookbindery was mostly "schoolboy drivel." When pressed to define "schoolboy drivel," Theodore Strauss said, "Girls and cars and pulp novels and Hollywood stars and such."

11. Sinclair Bowling gives a statement about Lee Harvey to the Warren Commission.

12. In which the man who sold Lee Harvey a guitar recounts that fateful day.

9. Lee Harvey's mother gives the world a piece of her mind regarding her son.

Marguerite Oswald—Lee Harvey's mother—when asked about her boy's time before he made his way into Russia, went on record saying, "Oh, yes, my son was always up in his room strumming the guitar. I'm glad you brought that up, because what nobody is saying about my son is that he was gifted. Don't ask me now to describe his gift. It is something spiritual that I can identify with because it's something I've always felt carrying, myself. And I always knew this spiritual thing was in Lee, because I'm his mother. I came all the way to Washington on my own dime to prove my son's innocence, and I'm glad you brought that up because the historical truth is that my son was a creative individual. He'd listen to his records up there so quietly all by himself. None of us was ever allowed up there when he was playing his records, and, yes, strumming his guitar. Now, I don't know about this Bowling boy, and I don't recall my son being employed at a bookbindery. Lee had so many jobs that it's a possibility. And as far as a musical duet named Sarcophagus? I suppose that's a possibility, too. Lee did love reading stories of when they dug up that Egyptian King Tut's grave. And the curse that came with the bargain. I am his mother and I know these details. I came all the way to Washington to deny all accusations against my son. To clear his name. And who is asking me how I'm paying my way? I have my living expenses, too, you know, while I continue touring the country advocating for my son. My son was a hero."

End.

10. In which Lee Harvey meets up again with Sinclair Bowling.

Walking the streets of downtown Dallas looking for a job one day, Lee Harvey ran into Sinclair Bowling, coincidentally, the same way they'd met. After hearing the unmistakable sound of a book dropping, Lee Harvey bent down, picked it up, and saw that the person it belonged to was Sinclair Bowling.

"Lee," Sinclair exclaimed, "you'll never believe this. I'm working at a radio station up the street. They put me in charge of Theater Hour in the afternoon, helping with the sound effects. Guess what they have in there? Not only an organ, but all sorts of instruments we could use, and props for theatrical sounds."

Bowling invited Lee Harvey to sit through a performance of *Bring My Heart, My Darling*. Afterward, for old times' sake, they acquired a fifth of schnapps and drank it in an alley, waiting for the station's white noise hours.

That night, they got into the radio station using Sinclair Bowling's key. Sitting in front of the keys of the piano organ, Bowling encouraged Lee Harvey to play the old chord progressions on the guitar, and to try using the washboard, wood blocks, and metal percussion instruments at his own discretion.

In a fit of inspiration, Bowling turned on the station's reel-to-reel and recorded that impromptu session.

13. Lee Harvey meets Sinclair Bowling, darkness hovers, then they forever part ways.
14. Lee Harvey and Sinclair Bowling share their bad luck, good fortune, then part.

11. Sinclair Bowling gives a statement about Lee Harvey to the Warren Commission.

Under deposition, Sinclair Bowling admitted that the first time he met Lee Harvey, he thought he was a jokester because Lee Harvey was wearing thick-rimmed glasses without the lenses. "So only the frames?" Earl Warren asked. "Yes," Bowling replied under oath, "only the frames." The day following that encounter, Lee Harvey showed up without the glasses and Bowling never thought to bring them up again.

Bowling said Lee Harvey was good for conversation, was a good listener, and, sure, he could talk about art, and, sure, he could strum a few chords, and, sure, they'd played together two, three, maybe four times and perhaps recorded, but there was a singular thing about Lee Harvey that people just didn't get: he had a talent with matches. Lee Harvey always carried a matchbox with him, and using a fine pocketknife, he'd carve the profile of a celebrity on every matchstick before striking it. You'd think it couldn't be done, that a matchstick doesn't have sufficient surface area for a person's profile. But Lee Harvey could do it. Bowling wanted to say that one of the profiles he'd carved was that of John Fitzgerald Kennedy, who'd won a Pulitzer Prize by then but was not quite president. However, upon being pressed on the matter, Bowling told Earl Warren he couldn't be sure.

End.

12. In which the man who sold Lee Harvey a guitar recounts that fateful day.

Out of those interviewed by the Warren Commission, the only person to shed light on the two Sarcophagus recordings was Griffith Acosta, proprietor of Texas Thrift and the man who ended up selling young Lee Harvey the guitar. Acosta went on record saying, "I remember him as a fidgety, anxious young man, but perhaps we're all a little of those things at that age. Was interested in chamber music and composers. The moment that stands out in my memory is Mr. Oswald asking how it was that one went from writing songs on a guitar to being orchestral. In short, he was asking how one became a composer. Think I answered like my father would answer, and said you become a composer the same way you become a doctor or a boxcar jumper. You jump a boxcar. You compose. You want to be a composer, start composing, or move toward composing. You want to be a boxcar jumper, jump a boxcar."

15. Time passes and people start hearing rumors of the Sarcophagus recordings.

16. An account of thieves making away with a Sarcophagus record.

13. Lee Harvey meets Sinclair Bowling, darkness hovers, then they forever part ways.

Jim's Restaurant. A rainy, gray Sunday morning.

Spooked and a little apprehensive, Lee Harvey agreed to meet Sinclair Bowling for breakfast before most people had made it out of church. They both had a bowl of oatmeal, toast, orange juice, and under the table passed each other a flask of gin that Bowling had brought. He was nervous and a little sad about letting Lee Harvey in on the news, so he waited until they were walking to Bowling's car in the parking lot.

There had been five records he'd paid to be pressed out of the reel-to-reel recordings they'd made at the station. However, Bowling said, he'd been fired and had failed to grab them before he was asked to leave, and had never returned. The records were still out there somewhere.

Lee Harvey and Sinclair Bowling walked along the edge of Amaranth Creek and Bowling said, "There's no room for people like me and you in this world, Lee. We know too much about how things operate. Society doesn't reward anybody that knows too much unless you're military. Or you go to the big colleges."

Lee Harvey slightly disagreed, and when they came to a consensus, Bowling said, "And what do we come to now, Lee? Men like you and me. If they don't let us survive by doing what we wanna be doing. By making music, and what's that? I guess art, too, yes. But what do we do, you ask? Well. We live our lives. As Americans. And maybe from the inside we can fight it back. How? By pretending to be good husbands, good fathers. Good patriots. And then one day by taking it down. Yeah. I hope somebody out there finds one of those records. And that they listen to them. Then history will remember something about us one day."

It started to drizzle and the young men parted. Sinclair Bowling never came across Lee Harvey Oswald in person again.

End.

14. Lee Harvey and Sinclair Bowling share their bad luck, good fortune, then part.

Lee Harvey started a job at a warehouse loading dock and quickly gained a reputation for letting his mind wander and doing sloppy work. While he was unloading a barrel of salt one morning, the dolly hit a pebble that caused the barrel to tip, and a pile of salt spilled in the middle of the warehouse. Lee Harvey was fired on the spot.

He was strolling through the part of Dallas called Old Riviera, clutching *Western Constructivism* by Chanier Rice and rereading excerpts, when suddenly right in front of him appeared Sinclair Bowling, walking in the opposite direction with a copy of *The Secret Rituals of Mankind Anthology*, edited by Marian B. Marcus. And what were the odds: Bowling had also just been fired from his job at the radio station. They'd caught him sneaking in at night after having made a mess of the studio one time.

"But look," Bowling said, and from a bag in his trench coat brought out five blank seven-inch records in sheer white sleeves. He handed two to Lee Harvey and confessed he'd made records of the time they'd played together at the station. These were the only existing copies and, personally, Bowling wanted three for himself.

The young men acquired a fifth of schnapps and drank it

in an alley downtown until a few hours before sundown. Bowling wished Lee Harvey luck, and they parted, looking forward to their next encounter.

As he waited for the bus, Lee Harvey held one of the record sleeves clumsily and a record fell to the sidewalk. Lee Harvey was shocked and dismayed to watch it break into four pieces.

Threatened by fate, Lee Harvey clutched the other record tightly as the bus approached.

When he boarded he told himself he had to be more careful, then paid the fare.

End.

15. Time passes and people start hearing rumors of the Sarcophagus recordings.

About twelve years after Oswald's death, in the winter issue of the Argentine avant-garde jazz quarterly *Tenebrarum*, Zik Fanti wrote about a fruitful trip to the United States in an article titled "Jazz in the Wind." In it, Fanti describes meeting a man named Griffith Acosta, who was the owner of Glitz, an experimental record shop in an artsy area of Chicago, and who once sold Oswald the only guitar he ever purchased. In the span of an afternoon, Acosta recounted to Fanti his life since "all that" (Acosta's preferred term for the murders of JFK and Lee Harvey and the subsequent aftermath).

At the time of his deposition with the Warren Commission, Acosta had sold both thrift shops he'd owned—it turned out that his brief exchange with Oswald, and being forced to recount their conversation over and over, had led Acosta to some inner searching. When Acosta came to the part of the story about how he left Texas and came to own a unique record shop in Chicago, he casually mentioned the resurfaced Sarcophagus recordings he'd cut for Lee Harvey and Bowling.

"So the recordings are real?" Fanti asked.

"Oh yes," replied Acosta.

16. An account of thieves making away with a Sarcophagus record.

Acosta said he had approached the government several times after finding the two Sarcophagus tracks he'd recorded back in '59, the only year he'd had access to that kind of equipment, since he was also part investor in a radio station. Acosta remembered doing only two takes of each song and that it was Lee Harvey—not Bowling—who had taken one of the records to keep. The other copy Acosta had kept for his own files, but, having sold his belongings and moved several times between then and '65, when he was under oath for Earl Warren and the other government officials, he'd lost it. Acosta knew that, given time, he would find it. When he finally did, the government no longer cared about those recordings. "They must've felt it had nothing to do with killing the president," Acosta said to a music journalist, Zik Fanti. Fanti, however, had no luck in being one of its few listeners: The record had been stolen seven months prior. The thieves hauled away the two-hundred-pound safe from Acosta's fortified back office and probably had no idea what was in there, just assumed it had to be valuable.

15. Time passes and people start hearing rumors of the Sarcophagus recordings.
19. Relating to how life manages to link us all.

17. Concerning Lee Harvey's daughter, and how we all cope.

Around this time, south of Houston, a twelve-year-old girl was living in her own fantasy world, where the other children came from an ice planet, and she'd been sent to this earth because her real parents were political dissidents back home. In the girl's fantasy, she was the only one who knew how to be loyal and patriotic, which is why at every school she attended kids eventually caught on and would stop her in the halls to tell her: "Your daddy killed our president." And those kids meant it—meant it because they had to mean it. The girl watched as their words became icicles, as everything the kids touched turned to purple rock crystal, and she could see tiny orange spiders running through their veins, stretching their skin. In the outside world she still had control of the army ants, and this comforted the girl. One day the ants would emerge as a cyclone, and when the kids were bitten all over they would remember that army ants live everywhere below the ground they walked on. When the girl got home she had supper with her earth family and afterward excused herself. She sat on her bed reading *Amazing Stories* with the phonograph headphones on, listening to the record she knew had once been her papa's.

End.

18. How the recordings found a place in history and became part of a movement.

Zik Fanti went on to become the would-be founder and director of the Academy of Avant-Garde Aesthetics, a secondary school in South America that would focus on the advancement of surrealist and avant-garde studies in its curriculum. Fanti and his investors believed that the study of surrealism and all its branches—including but not limited to Dadaism, perspectivism, unthinkism, and folktales, along with abstract concepts of music—made a society more proactive and aware of its own problems and their possible solutions. The concept of history would be taught through exploring pockets of national and world literature, and they'd read work by Zoe Zuchmayer, Bishop Zürn, Anna Kavan, and Sagawa Chika, as well as medieval manuscripts and apocryphal texts, and would study questionable historical documents like the Voynich manuscript, photographs of cave paintings, and Edgar More's *Beyond Utopia*. They'd also have to learn by heart the *Tractatus Logico-Philosophicus*; the most scathing essays by Suppleton, Elizabeth Chapman, and George Laye; and Valerie Solanas's *SCUM Manifesto*. On top of all this, students would have to be familiar with the lives of María Claude, Oscar Terra, Emma Butler, and every artist in the rentism movement. The academy would have a library of old 78 rpm shellac records that would include some of the earliest recordings ever created, and an extensive collection of experiments in minimalism, discord, and dissonance, along with works by Truman Glass, Pauline Oliveros, Albert Ayler, Béla Bartók, Scott Joplin, Anatoly Lyadov, Igor Stravinsky, Mary Lou Williams, Juventino Rosas, and all the greats. Along with regional recordings put out by the Quarto Kinto record label like *Czech-Mex: Experiments with Horns and Accordions*, *The Big Secret Anthology*, and *Nuggets: Tripped Out Artyfacts*, there would be an unlabeled record in a sheer white sleeve, both mysterious and special. In this academy, all students would be required to know all these works. But then the markets in several countries crashed, banks went bust, investors pulled, and Fanti's academy never took off.

End.

19. Relating to how life manages to link us all.

Sometime in the early nineties a young, lazy-eyed boy in the checkpoint town of Falfurrias, Texas, was running through an orange grove pretending to be a soldier in a great war, when not very far from him, actual shots rang out. The boy ran back home, fearing the worst. On the front porch of his grandmother's two-story adobe home, the boy's mother sat sobbing while his father held back tears, with a red face, his shotgun by his side. The boy was guided by his mother to the hospice room in the house—after a prolonged sickness, his grandmother Magda had finally passed.

Family from as far away as Durango and Chicago attended the modest funeral at the Mexican pantheon in Falfurrias. An Old World–style celebration of Abuelita Magda's life and legacy ensued at her adobe home until the following day, filled with dancing, carne asada, menudo, and a spread of gourmet pan dulce.

When Abuelita Magda's phonograph and dismal record collection were discovered, it allowed the distant cousins from Durango and Chicago to break through their language barrier and bond over the music. They listened to boleros, polkas, classical compositions, and then they came across a smaller record. Instead of a label, on one side, scratched very fine, were the words THIS AND THAT, and on the opposite side the words ONE PLUS ONE DON'T MAKE TWO. They put it on and listened to it with as much curiosity, enthusiasm, and patience as they had to the other records. A drone emerged from the mouth of the phonograph like an acidic smell—an unamplified voice echoed, like a ghost trying to groan with its face pressed against glass—an untuned guitar swung like a pendulum—then the fuzzy night made its way out of the mouth. All the cousins' expressions held a mixture of frowns and laughter. "What kind of stuff was Abuelita listening to," one of them asked out loud.

20. Fin.

20. Fin.

Outside, a toddler in braids held tightly to her bag of marbles, suspicious of all the boys, and tried not to flinch when the fireworks went *pop-pop, pop-pop*.

ACKNOWLEDGMENTS

These stories were drafted between 2010 and January 2020, either on an Olivetti Underwood Lettera 32 or on regular notebook paper, while I was working in the food industry or as a bookseller to make money. My coworkers and artist friends throughout these years made the most tedious moments tolerable, even enjoyable, and I'd like to thank each of them, regardless if we may not speak like we used to, in no particular order. So thanks to Stephanie Hannay, Barrett Barnard, Chea Serda, Travis McGuire, Schandra Madha, Matthew Hodges, Annar Veröld, Stephanie Goehring, Taylor Pate, Angel Serda, Marcos Jorge, Stephen Vogel, Will Schmidt, Felipe Granados, Elias Serda, Weston Young, Timmy Martin, Rebecca Rippon, Tony Castillo, Clayton Lillard, Julie Poole, Markus Armstrong, Leda and Chantal Ginestra, Christina Lough, Travis Cumbo, Adrian Whipp, Loren Doyen, Justin Delgado, Bryan Hilton, John Johnson, Eric Morales, Lauren Sweet, Phil Lovegren, Leslie Scott, Alicia Bowling, Ruth Lashbrook, Devin James Fry, Adrianne Francini, Claire Bowman, Grace Marlow, Kristopher Ohlinger, Stephanie Mueller, Douglas Marshall, MTN, Kana Harris, Stuart Scott, Jonathan Oropeza, Josh Permenter, Danielle Burgess, Chad Hopper, Amanda Jones, Billy Baca, Christopher Hutchins, and pretty much anybody who ever worked at Longhorn Po-Boys & Falafel and Lava Java.

I am lucky and grateful to have my two sisters, Anna and Alba, and lucky to have my father, so a big thank-you to each of them. Lots of love to my mother, forever. Grateful for my family in Texas, Reynosa, Monterrey, and elsewhere, and for my cousins Rubén and Eduardo and José Carlos.

I could never thank my agent, Soumeya B. Roberts, enough, but thank you, Soumeya.

Thank you, Elva Baca, James Graham, and Ramona. Thank you, Jim Mendiola (watch his classic Chicano film *Pretty Vacant*, and pretty much anything else by him). Thanks to Maria Topete and Cruz Angeles for the encouragement in my very early years, and for their films, which I also recommend. Thank you, Raúl Castillo, for your friendship and art these past twenty years.

Thanks to my RGV people: Derek Beltran, Amanda Elise Salas, Kirsten Alyssa Salas, Carl and Sofia Vestweber, Fred Garcia, the Bunnyman, Jim Lloyd, and anyone who ever "junkyarded" in the alley behind 10th Street Café/Athena's Coffee Shop between the years 2002 and 2004.

Thanks to Marc Villareal and We Suck, who later changed their name to the Malcontent Party: RGV legends on par with Bill Burroughs, they inspired a whole generation of kids like me during that crucial first G. W. Bush term.

Thanks to all the journals and literary magazines where these stories initially appeared in different versions, especially to Andrew Durbin and Medaya Ocher for reaching out as editors. Thanks to Chris Gannon, Chadwick Wood, and the team at Wander, for inviting me on and providing the map that served as the structure for "The Oswald Variations." Thanks especially to Leyla Shams, whose idea it was to bring me aboard; thanks to Amelia Kreminski, who worked on it.

Thank you to the book-world friends I've made during this time, especially mónica teresa ortiz, Raquel Gutiérrez, J. David Gonzalez,

Dobby Gibson, Daley Farr, Corey Miller, Bing Li, Madeline ffitch, Uriel Perez, and Mark Haber.

Thanks to Little Max, who was present during the drafting of every one of these stories, and may he rest in peace. I miss you every day, my friend.

I listened to Courtney Barnett's cover of "Shivers" on repeat during the writing of "You Got It, Take It Away," so thank you, Courtney Barnett, for taking me there. Nat King Cole's "El Bodeguero" straight-up inspired "Pheasants," and I played it very loud while writing it, so thank you for everything, Nat King Cole, especially for those Spanish records.

Thanks to the labels Unseen Worlds, Mississippi Records, and Light in the Attic for the necessary jams. Thanks to my local record stores: Bluebonnet Records, Breakaway Records, and End of an Ear.

Thanks to my local and not-so-local indie bookstores: BookPeople, Book Woman, Brazos Bookstore, Pilsen Community Books, Point Reyes Books, Skylight Books, City Lights Bookstore, Deep Vellum Books, the Center for Fiction, Third Place Books, Riffraff Bookstore, and, of course, Becky Garcia, Joe, and the crew at Malvern Books.

Special thanks to all the booksellers out there, too.

As if all this was not enough, a mountain range of thanks is reserved for my visionary editor, Jackson Howard, and the entire team behind the scenes at MCD × FSG Originals, including, but not limited, to: Chloe Texier-Rose, Na Kim, June Park, Mitzi Angel, and Sean McDonald. I'd also like to thank Caitlin Van Dusen, Emily Bell, Danny Vazquez, and Naomi Huffman.

Lastly, thanks to Adira and Taisia K. I'd be nothing without these two. And that's for damn sure.